TEARS OF THE BUFFALO

The days of slaughtering buffalo are meant to be over, with so pitifully few of them remaining. But with top dollar on offer for their severed heads as trophies, some hunters just can't resist. In Yellowstone Park, Captain Moses Harris and his company of US Cavalry are assigned the job of stopping illegal poachers. Yet, following an apparently motiveless murder at the Mammoth army post, Harris realizes that it is not only the buffalo being threatened by greed and corruption . . .

PAUL BEDFORD

◆

TEARS OF THE BUFFALO

Complete and Unabridged

Paul Bedford (signature)

LINFORD
Leicester

First published in Great Britain in 2018 by
Robert Hale
an imprint of The Crowood Press
Wiltshire

First Linford Edition
published 2022
by arrangement with The Crowood Press
Wiltshire

A catalogue record for this book is available
from the British Library.

ISBN 978-1-4448-4877-9

Published by
Ulverscroft Limited
Anstey, Leicestershire

Printed and bound in Great Britain by
TJ Books Ltd., Padstow, Cornwall

This book is printed on acid-free paper

To Denise G. Marsden.
Many thanks for supporting my writing
efforts over the years.

1

The First Day

'I don't know if those big shaggies can cry, but they're sure entitled!' Charlie Allard had to partially shield his eyes from the brilliantly sunlit snow, but he could still make out the pitifully few creatures in the valley below.

'Yeah,' Deke Wilson replied softly. 'It's a *cry*ing shame what the white man's done to them.' So saying, he hefted his heavy Sharps buffalo gun to a more sustainable position. It was entirely possible that the two men would have to wait a long time before they made their move, because any action depended upon the arrival of a certain Frank Potts. And he was known to be a notoriously tricky and unpredictable individual!

Yellowstone Park, located mostly in the Territory of Wyoming, was a place of stark beauty in the winter months. Although many summer visitors might be struck by the sheer splendour of the national park, those of honest intent mostly kept well clear in the cold season, because then it was all about survival. The temperature stubbornly remained well below freezing, and deep snow covered everything except in the immediate vicinity of the geysers and hot springs. One would have thought that in such conditions the few surviving animals would at least be safe from human predators, but the opposite was true. Buffalo grew a thick winter coat that made their hides even more valuable, and the snow made it almost impossible for them to flee. And sadly, as a sign of changing times, their body parts were also much sought after as souvenirs. The head of a now rare buffalo was worth a great many silver dollars to collectors back east. Such was the way of the world in 1887.

* * *

'He's here!' Allard whispered sharply.
    Wilson jumped slightly as he came

to his senses. The low sun had moved across the sky. Much time had passed, but as on so many occasions nowadays he had been wrapped up in his own dark thoughts, and had forgotten just how freezing it was. Such careless behaviour could get a man killed. He knew of people so numbed by cold that they had unwittingly drifted off and never woken again. 'Where away?' he inquired quickly.

'Off to the right, down behind those trees.'

Wilson stared hard down into the stretch of valley below their position on the side of Mount Wood. Located in the extreme northeastern section of the park, on what was almost a peninsula surrounded by non-parkland, it had a creek running through it that was a ready source of water . . . when it didn't freeze. He grunted with satisfaction. 'I see the son of a bitch. Want me to drop him?' he asked eagerly. 'It'd be no trouble, an' then I could maybe move onto the shaggies,' he added wistfully.

Allard regarded him sadly for a

moment. 'For Christ's sake, Deke, just accept what the captain said. There's to be no killing. Of anything. He says those days are gone. That there's hardly any buffalo left now, and it's our job to protect them. An' in case you hadn't noticed, he's the boss.'

'So *why* did you ask him to send me with you, then?'

Allard's expression changed, so that he was now favouring the other man with a lopsided smile. 'Because, like you, there's just too many folks can't give up the old ways. And I don't aim to take a bullet just to keep some officer happy. So when I move down there to arrest him, peaceably like, you stay up here and cover me. Once I've disarmed him, you can follow me down. If it don't pan out, and you *have* to use that cannon, just try not to hurt him bad. Remember, we've all got a long haul out of here to Mammoth.' So saying, he got to his feet, strapped on his skis and began to move crabwise down the hillside. The ten-feet long wooden skis attached to his boots, stopped him from sinking into the deep powdery snow, and allowed him to make good speed. Their undersides were greased with tallow to aid progress on cross-country marches.

Wilson had to admit that, for a mere soldier, the other man had chosen their position well. While he remained concealed behind some rocks, Allard was able to descend using a screen of lodgepole pines as cover. Their prey, solely intent upon stalking the buffalo, apparently had no inkling that he, too, was being hunted. Sighing, the scout carefully eased his Sharps through a convenient cranny in the rocks and drew a bead on their prospective prisoner. He knew all too well that if he were to ignite the 110 grains of black powder in its monstrous cartridge, he could effortlessly despatch Potts straight to hell. Yet, of course, he wasn't permitted to do that. The stream of black tobacco juice that he spat out showed just what he thought of such restrictive conditions. Then, abruptly, everything changed.

'Oh, Christ! He's got a dog.'

* * *

Frank Potts broke cover at speed, his greased skis moving smoothly over the virgin powder. The sled carrying his few 'possibles' had been left behind in the trees. He was unconcerned that the big, dumb animals might see him, because it really didn't matter. In such conditions they simply had no chance of outrunning him. All they could do was flounder a few paces in the deep snow. And the fact that he could close in on them, more or less at leisure, meant that he didn't need some big expensive Sharps, with its big expensive cartridges that could hit like a freight train from over a mile away. At point blank range, even his ancient but very reliable Spencer Carbine would do the job . . . if one knew which part of the massive body to hit. It was a sad truth though, that rimfire cartridges weren't so easy to come by nowadays.

So swift and silent was his progress that Potts got within some twenty yards of the nearest buffalo before it registered his presence. The great beast snorted loudly as a warning to the others in the stand. Then, desperately, it tried to escape. On the Great Plains, baked hard by summer sun, it would have been off at a tremendous pace, leaving the hunter to curse ineffectually, but not in Yellowstone in the depths of winter.

Being right-handed, Potts swerved to a halt, so that his left shoulder faced the fleeing creature. He was then able to un-sling the carbine from its resting place across his back and take swift aim for a disabling shot. Cocking the hammer, he closed his left eye and peered down the open sights at the frantic animal's left hip. That would do nicely. His right forefinger curled around the trigger and . . .

From back near the pine trees, his dog barked. It wasn't a playful bark, because Cody wasn't given to such things, and in any case knew better than to spoil a kill.

7

He was sounding the alarm. With the hairs up on the back of his neck, Potts attempted to swing around to meet the unexpected threat, but the damned skis hampered his movements. His head was able to react quicker than the rest of his body. Consequently, he saw the unknown figure racing towards him, but was unable to immediately draw a bead on him. Not so his dog, however.

Cody was some sort of mixed breed, jet black and contrasting sharply with the rather cosy name endowed by his master. From the look of him, he could easily have been part wolf, with a strain of pure malevolence running through him. Although up against the same deep snow that so hampered the buffalo, he was powerfully muscled and far, far lighter. And so, for a short stretch, he was able to bound at great speed towards the stranger approaching his master. His teeth were bared, ready to clamp down on vulnerable tendons.

Charlie Allard heard the barking as he was in full flow towards his prey. Both hands held the single pole that he used to propel himself forward. His only weapon was the government issue Colt Single Action Army revolver, tucked away in an enclosed holster, strapped to the belt around his waist. Having been in apparent control of the situation, he now found himself in mortal danger from two separate sources. It would only be moments before Potts got his Spencer pointing at him, and the goddamned hound could even be faster than that. There really was no alternative. Sliding to a halt, he dropped the pole and turned side on, so as to both present a narrower target to the poacher, and to see just what was pursuing him.

'Sweet Jesus,' he exclaimed, as his gloved hands fumbled frantically with the regulation flap holster. He wasn't going to make it, and he knew it! The vicious-looking animal, with its great jaws open and ready, was almost on him. Discarding the pole had been a big mistake, because he could at least have used it to fend the creature off. Even as his hand closed around the butt of his revolver, the dog launched itself at his throat.

From high up on the hillside, there came a tremendous roar, almost like a minor explosion. In mid-flight, the terrifying canine was quite literally flung to one side, blood pumping from the hole in its belly. It was very obvious that the creature would pose no further threat . . . ever.

Twisting around to face the poacher, Allard got his revolver clear of its holster, and thumbed back the hammer. He fully expected to be forced to use it, but found to his relief that such was not the case. Potts appeared deflated, as though suddenly robbed of any desire to resist. As he stared dejectedly at the blood-drenched animal twitching in its death throes, his Spencer's muzzle dropped until it brushed the snow, no longer a menace to either man or beast.

'You'd got no call killing Cody,' he blurted out accusingly.

Allard blinked with surprise. 'What

the hell kind of name's that for a dog?'

'I visited with Buffalo Bill once, and took a liking to him. Not that it's got anything to do with you,' Potts retorted angrily, before adding, 'Just who the hell are you, anyhu?'

The other man gestured with his Colt. 'The howdy dos can wait. First off, you'd better ease the hammer down on that carbine, very careful like. Then throw it over towards me. Then we'll parley. And remember, there's a sharpshooter back of me got you squarely in his sights!'

Only after Potts had complied did the soldier unbutton his bearskin momentarily to reveal the blue tunic underneath. 'Sergeant Allard, Company M, 1st Cavalry. I'm arresting you for breaking Park Order Number Five.' He paused for a moment to get the words right in his head. 'It forbids hunting or trapping, or the discharge of firearms within the park.'

'I didn't know I was in the park, and nor did I discharge any damn firearms,' Potts protested. 'But your sidekick sure

11

as hell did! An' I ain't after any trophy heads or hides, neither. I'm hunting for food, and there shouldn't be any law agin that! That's why I've got a sled over yonder, to haul the meat back.'

The non-commissioned officer regarded him with professional curiosity. 'A beast the size of a buffalo. Now how's one man fixing to eat all that meat? You must have a mighty powerful hunger on you.'

'Well, shucks, it ain't all for me,' the poacher protested. 'There's others waiting on it.'

'What others?'

Potts opened his mouth to respond, but then promptly thought better of it. Only after pondering for a moment did he reply. 'You ain't getting anything more out of me, soldier boy.'

★ ★ ★

It was some time before Deke Wilson joined the two men. Only once he was satisfied that the non-com was in control

12

of the situation did he begin his descent, with the single spent cartridge case tucked away in his pocket for future use. His arrival was greeted with a nod of gratitude from the soldier, and an entirely predictable display of sullen hostility from Frank Potts.

'You killed my dog, you cockchafer! That big gun of yours plumb tore him to pieces.'

The animal had by now indeed passed away, but Wilson was entirely unrepentant. 'Only felons have dogs you can't see at night!'

Potts chewed thoughtfully on his bottom lip. This newcomer quite obviously had some hard bark on him, and a trusty Sharps to back it up. He knew what their intentions were, but also possessed a surprisingly sentimental side that meant he wasn't for cooperating quite yet. 'I ain't leaving 'til Cody's buried,' he announced abruptly, following it with an even more foolish pronouncement. 'An' you can't make me.'

Allard shook his head emphatically.

'No deal, mister. The ground is iron hard, an' we ain't waiting around for the spring thaw. We're taking you before Captain Harris in Mammoth, and the dog stays where he lays.'

Potts drew a deep breath into his scrawny frame. 'Well, then, I will not go! What do you say to that?'

Wilson had already heard more than enough. Somehow, the muzzle of his Sharps was directed abruptly at the poacher's groin. 'Mister, you either come with us under your own steam, or we'll strap you to your sled and drag you back. But to show our displeasure, first off we'll tie you to one of them pines and beat you to a pulp for the trouble you've caused.' As he spoke, his eyes were like flints. There could be no doubting his intent. 'How's that grab you?'

A beaten look came into Potts's shifty eyes, but there was more grief to come because then his tormenter pulled a set of wrist irons into view.

'You ain't putting them shackles on me like I'm some common criminal!'

Wilson expelled an exaggerated sigh. 'Now, there you go again: talk, talk, talk. These are just for your own good, because if you took it on yourself to try to escape, I'd have to blow a big hole in you . . . just like I did for your dog. You wouldn't want that now, would you?'

Potts glared at him with real hatred, but nevertheless proffered his hands.

'Good for you,' Wilson remarked easily. 'I knew you'd see the sense of it.'

* * *

Darkness was beginning to fall as the six men moved in a group along the valley floor. All of them were on skis and were unencumbered by any sleds. Instead, four of them carried various poles and carefully packaged instruments strapped across their backs. The individual at the rear had a heavily greased repeating rifle slung over his shoulder. They had come into this particular section of the vast park from the southeast, and seemed to possess a pretty fair idea of the lie of the land. Yet they would need far more than that if they were to make it back to Cooke City, because with the fading light came a bone-chilling cold that was already intensifying. Anyone remaining in the open without a fire would be unlikely to survive the night.

'I'm telling you, that little shit has run out on us,' one of them opined bitterly through the muffler around his pinched features.

Another shook his head adamantly. 'I ain't gain-saying that he's a little shit, but Frank Potts doesn't run out on anybody.'

'So where is he, then?' demanded a third.

A tall man, with prematurely greying hair under his thick woollen hood, slowed down abruptly and waved them all to silence. Quite obviously their leader, he'd spotted a dark object in the snow that just didn't look right. Angling his skis, he made straight for it. The dead dog, coated in frozen blood from the large bullet wound, told part of the story. The rest of the tale would have to be filled out by the various tracks in the snow.

'Looks like its health just plumb gave out,' someone remarked with a snigger. 'I reckon Frank'll be supping from the cup of sorrow tonight. He really loved that dumb mutt.'

'If that's the best you can come up with, Carter, hold your tongue,' the tall individual snapped. 'Tatum, take a look around. Tell me what happened here.'

'Sure thing, Mister Lomax,' answered the man with the Winchester.

'The rest of you spread out and stay alert.'

As the others complied, Tatum inspected the corpse first, before expanding his search to take in the nearest trees. Unlike the others, who had the look of only occasional frontiersmen, he possessed features that appeared to be etched with years of exposure and hard experience. It didn't take him long to figure out just what had occurred.

'It was some kind of buffalo gun

done for that critter. Big bore, and very powerful. Sort of piece a professional would carry.'

'Professional what?'

The other man shrugged. 'There's a limit to what you can learn from tracks, Mister Lomax. What I *can* say is this: two men were waiting for Potts. He's a known poacher of buffalo and anything else on four legs. Some cuss might have informed on him, or possibly he just got unlucky. His sled is still over in those pines. The sharpshooter killed his dog from somewhere on the side of that mountain, whilst his partner made the arrest. Since the animal was likely moving fast, I'd say it was damn good shooting. Anyhu, the shooter then came down here to join the others. After that, all three headed off to the west. Since there's nothing else over that way other than the army post at Mammoth, I reckon the other fellow was a blue belly. 'Cause that's the main reason the army's here, to stop poaching. Although I don't reckon they'd take too kindly to us if they knew what you fellas was up to.'

Lomax stared at his tracker intently for a moment, before spitting an impressive clump of yellow phlegm angrily in the direction of Cody's unresponsive body. 'Shit. If Potts talks, he could jeopardize the whole scheme.'

The other man who claimed knowledge of the poacher spoke up. 'Mister Lomax, I don't rightly know what jeopardise means, but I know Frank Potts. He won't talk. I'd wager specie on that.'

'I hear you, Carter, but I can't take that chance,' their boss retorted sharply. 'If any government employee gets wind of what we've been doing, then all this is for nought.' He stood in his skis for a while, lost in thought. Four of his employees knew better than to interrupt him, and Tatum had already said his piece. Finally, Lomax came to a decision. 'We'll camp over in those trees for the night. Get a proper fire going using Potts' sled and skin that dog. Along with beans and beef jerky, we should get a decent meal. Come first light, we're making for Mammoth. There's business there that needs attending to.'

'Pity your phlegm missed that critter,' Tatum remarked drily. 'Might have given it a bit of seasoning.'

2

The Second Day

Captain Moses Harris felt a fleeting glow of satisfaction as the prisoner was locked in the single-room shack that passed for the guardhouse. Only *fleeting*, because he knew full well that until Congress passed the necessary legislation, the US Army had no legal right to detain poachers and other undesirables arrested in Yellowstone. Officially, all he could do as the park's military superintendent was confiscate their supplies and eject them from its environs. But Mammoth's very isolation meant that the captain was a great distance away from any higher authority. The telegraph didn't count, of course, because it was entirely up to him whether he chose to use it, and so he fully intended to stretch the letter of the law a little. This damned scoundrel, Potts, could at least cool his heels under lock and key for a couple of days before they sent him on his way. Quite literally, in fact, since there wasn't any form of heating in the building.

'Wilson, Sergeant,' he acknowledged, as the two men approached to offer their report. 'Well done, both of you. Did he give you any trouble?'

Allard favoured his superior with a wry smile. 'Not especially, but his dog did . . . and paid the price.'

Harris felt a surge of pleasure. Some animals needed killing. 'Really? Good for you. It might just give him pause next time he considers hunting in the park. Then again, probably not. Some folks really can't change. Anything else to report, before you get a well-earned hot meal and some rest?'

The sergeant shrugged. 'It may be nothing, sir, but Potts did mention one thing that didn't sit right. He seemed to reckon that the meat from any buffalo kill was meant to feed some other fellas in the park. When I tried to get more out of him, he just clammed up tight.'

The officer's eyebrows rose in surprise.

'Is that so? Well, in that case, I might just have a chinwag with him before we throw him out. This isn't the weather for casual visitors.'

'Shall I unlock the door for you, sir?' his non-com queried.

Harris glanced around at the failing light. The three men had got in just before nightfall, and already the cold was bitter and penetrating. 'No, I reckon not, thank you, Sergeant. We'll let him freeze his tail off until the morrow. The thought of more nights in there without any food might well loosen his tongue.' He chuckled and turned away. That Potts might be a tough little son of a bitch, but he certainly wouldn't forget his time in Mammoth as a guest of the army!

★ ★ ★

Darkness had fallen completely at the end of a very gruelling day by the time the shadowy figures had the army post in sight. With little need for any kind of defensive stockade, it merely consisted

23

of a group of rough-cut timber buildings of varying sizes. Snow coated the entire landscape and, without a breath of wind, there was an eerie stillness to the air. With the temperature way below freezing, the sight of two flickering pitch torches in amongst the structures only increased the men's yearning for warmth. The one consolation was that on such a night there was no armed guard patrolling the perimeter. With the various surviving Indian tribes much diminished and no longer a credible threat, such a punishing duty served no good purpose.

'Sweet Jesus, what I wouldn't give for one of those fire sticks? It's colder than a witch's tit out here,' Carter announced noisily.

Ben Lomax turned on him angrily. 'Shut your mouth, you damn fool,' he hissed. 'Sound travels too well in these conditions.' As the other man eyed him sullenly, Lomax switched his attention to Tatum. 'How many of us will go with you?'

The frontiersman glanced scornfully

around at the others before replying softly. 'It don't take but one blade to end a life, and I don't reckon any of this bunch would have the sand for it anyhu.' Then he peered up speculatively at his tall employer. '*You* might could manage it though, if his back was turned. You've got the look.' If Tatum realized he'd just given an insult, he didn't show it, and quite probably wouldn't have cared. There was a hard edge to him that none of the others could match. He was greedy, too! 'And you realize this is gonna cost plenty extra? I didn't sign on for no man killings.'

Although Lomax's eyes narrowed slightly, he offered no contradiction to any of the remarks. Instead, he merely answered mildly, 'Fair enough. We'll wait for you in those pines over yonder.'

Without another word, the assassin moved off towards the silent army post. Travelling slowly, he scrutinised the various buildings, weighing up which one might contain the incarcerated poacher. Knowing that there were unlikely to be many prisoners in such a place, he decided that it had to be one of three obviously single-roomed structures. Then, as he swept closer, Tatum noticed a door with an iron grill across its upper section. In spite of the biting chill, his hard features contorted into the semblance of a smile. That meant the other two, located on the periphery of the post, had to be shithouses.

Coming to a halt, he freed his feet from the skis. For what he had in mind, he would need freedom of movement. Glancing around, he saw that all the buildings were in darkness. Satisfied that he was unobserved, Tatum struck out for the jail. Immediately he sank deeper into the snow, but his progress was tolerable over a short distance. And then, quite suddenly, he was clear of it. A fatigue detail of soldiers had obviously been at work with shovels.

After removing his gloves, he approached the cell door until his face was almost touching the iron grill. Quietly, he extracted a vicious looking long-bladed hunting knife from its sheath. The gnarled ivory handle was curved and fitted his grip perfectly. With a grim smile of anticipation, he used it to tap gently on one of the bars. 'Yo, Potts. You in there?' he whispered.

For a long moment, the silence remained absolute, and then there were scuffling sounds on the floor inside. There was just enough moonlight to illuminate the perished features of the startled inmate. 'Sweet Jesus,' he croaked. 'You've actually come for me.'

'That I have,' Tatum replied quietly. 'An' you need to work with me if you're to get out of here. So get your ugly face up to these bars an' listen good.'

As Frank Potts stepped forward eagerly, the misery of his freezing incarceration fell from him like a cloak. He was going to have the last laugh on those poxy soldier boys after all. With his nose literally pressed against one of the bars, he awaited his rescuer's next words. That man opened his mouth as though to speak, and then performed two completely unexpected actions. His left hand snaked through the bars and seized hold of a clump of Potts's greasy hair. Almost simultaneously, the long blade of Tatum's knife jabbed forward through the grill and neatly skewered his victim's throat. Impaled on the cold steel, Potts briefly shuddered with shock, but was held in a vicelike grip. He tried to cry out, but no sound came. Then, even as warm blood soaked his right hand, the assassin coolly and deliberately twisted the blade. He knew well that he would only get the one opportunity at this, so he was taking no chances. Besides which, he was actually quite enjoying himself!

★ ★ ★

Even as Private Lane Turner curled up in a foetal position in an effort to ease his discomfort, he recognized that he was merely delaying the inevitable. His guts had been churning ever since he and the other enlisted men had turned

28

in, and there was really only one way to deal with it. There was a piss pot at the end of the barrack room, but that certainly wouldn't answer for his needs. He knew that he would just have to brave the bitter cold and pay a visit to the privy.

'God damn it all to hell,' he muttered as, with great reluctance, he flung aside the heavy blankets and clambered unhappily from his cot. Even with an iron stove at each end of the building the chill was disagreeable, but it would be nothing compared to that which awaited him outside.

After pulling on his freezing boots, Turner wrapped a thick coat over his long johns and crept to the door. With his comrades snoring behind him, he eased it open quietly and stepped out into the icy air. Trembling with cold, he almost had second thoughts, but then the grippes began again . . . only far more violently. Suddenly, nothing else mattered other than getting to the privy.

★ ★ ★

As Pott's lifeless body hit the hard-packed dirt floor there had been a muffled thump, closely followed by the sound of a door shutting nearby. Tatum, whose whole body tingled with reaction to the kill, was taken by surprise. Surely the two noises couldn't be connected? He had been about to crouch down near a patch of snow so as to clean the blood from both his hand and blade. Instead, he pressed his body back against the cell door and waited.

By great ill fortune, Private Turner's frantic outing to one of the most isolated buildings on the post took him right past the front of the guardhouse. As he approached it, with his sphincter muscle clenched tight, he abruptly became aware of a bulky figure lurking in front of the door. Preoccupied with his own troubles, Turner half-raised an arm in instinctive greeting. On such a night, it simply never occurred to him that some unknown intruder might mean him harm. And so it was that any chance of saving his own life had now passed.

Using the building behind him for leverage, Tatum launched himself towards the hastily advancing enlisted man. Coincidences counted for nothing in his harsh existence. All he knew was that an unexpected complication had to be dealt with . . . permanently. Consequently, his already blood-coated blade plunged deep into his opponent's stomach. Before that doomed individual could cry out, the assassin's horny hand clamped over his mouth. Then, under Tatum's greater momentum, the two men crashed to the hard ground, but of course it was Turner who took the brunt of it. With the air smashed from his lungs and a great steel blade twisting mercilessly in his belly, his end came quickly.

As all movement beneath him finally ceased, Tatum pulled his knife free with an audible sucking noise. Although maintaining the grip over his victim's mouth for a little longer, he clambered off the body and began to wipe his blade clean on the man's coat. That done, he took a long look around before finally sheathing it. The army post, with its flickering torchlight, was aptly as silent as a grave.

Instead of retreating immediately, he chuckled and patted the dead soldier playfully on one cheek. He never liked to rush his pleasures, and was in any case tempted by the possible contents of the man's pockets. Then his nose began to twitch under the assault of something very unpleasant. Glancing down at the long john-covered nether regions, he quickly saw what that *something* was.

'You dirty bastard,' he muttered, getting to his feet rapidly. Robbing the dead had suddenly lost its appeal, and with nothing else in Mammoth of interest it was definitely time to be on his way!

* * *

Ben Lomax waited impatiently as the hired hand took his own sweet time rejoining them under the snow-covered trees. Although he recognized that the man was checking his back trail very sensibly, he was keen to be off and didn't like to be kept waiting. Apart from any other considerations, he'd had a belly full of the unrelentingly piercing cold. And there was also something else gnawing at him that just wouldn't go away. What if all this skulduggery was for nothing? What if they were too late and Potts had already talked?

'Well?' he demanded, as the other man finally stood before him. 'Did you get it done?'

There was a strange glint in Tatum's eyes as that man replied. 'Yeah. Yeah, I did . . . and a little else besides.'

His employer didn't care for riddles. 'Just what exactly does that mean?'

'One of the soldier boys got in my way,' Tatum replied matter-of-factly. 'I had to see to him as well.'

Lomax felt as though his body temperature had plummeted suddenly. 'Jesus Christ! Do you realize what that could mean? Killing a low-life poacher was one thing, but a soldier!'

Tatum shrugged. His apparent indifference was unnerving. 'It was just plain bad luck, is all. He picked the wrong time to go for a shit, although I sent him to hell unburdened by that need, . . . Ha-ha. You can have him for free, though. I'll only charge for Potts.'

Lomax was struggling to control his temper, but he knew better than to lose it in the middle of nowhere in the company of such an obviously dangerous man. A sarcastic, 'That's mighty generous of you,' was the most he allowed himself, before turning to the others. 'We need to get well clear of here before making camp for the rest of the night. Then tomorrow we return to Cooke City. I've found out all I need to about this goddamn park.' He couldn't resist one more minor thrust at his assassin. 'I just hope that knife of yours hasn't ruined all our survey work.'

Tatum was totally unrepentant. It was as though a line had been crossed, and that being called on to carry out murder had subtly altered the relationship between him and his employer. 'I did what I had to do. If that blue belly had seen my face he could have fingered us all. As it is, all they got is two dead bodies. And frozen ones at that. Instead of bitching, you ought to be giving me a bonus!' With that, he turned his skis to the east and set off. The others had little choice other than to follow, if for no other reason than because Tatum was the only one who knew the exact way back.

Ben Lomax was barely aware of his actions as he worked the long pole in the snow. His mind was a seething morass as he weighed up the possible consequences of their deeds that night. What if the army gave chase? Jesus Christ, he was back to the 'what if's' again! One thing was for sure. He had a nasty feeling that he would regret this whole business!

3

The Third Day

Captain Harris stared in contemplative silence at the two corpses before him. He didn't give a damn about Potts's gory demise, but the visceral death of Private Turner affected him deeply, and was something that he took personally. The young soldier had been gutted like a fish, for God's sake. Since the passing of the Indian Wars, the killing of an enlisted man in any fashion was a comparative rarity, and such a thing could not be allowed to stand.

'Why all this killing?' Mammoth's commanding officer finally demanded, somewhat unreasonably, of Deke Wilson. 'Why not just set Potts free?'

That man had already scouted the area surrounding the army post, and had come to certain conclusions. 'Five of them waited in the trees over yonder, while one man did the killing. Whoever it was would have made too much noise smashing the lock to get Potts out. An' maybe they didn't want to be seen with him again, anyway. Not after we'd picked him up. There's also the fact that they were probably worried he'd talk. Anyhu, once the assassin had rejoined them, they all took off to the east. I reckon they're heading for Cooke City. The real question is what were they up to in Yellowstone that's worth killing folks over?'

'It's a question that I mean to have answered,' Harris remarked grimly. 'I know you and Sergeant Allard only came back in yesterday, but you're the most experienced men on the post, so I need the two of you to lead the hunt for those black-hearted rogues.'

The army scout peered at him curiously. 'Do we have any jurisdiction outside of the park, captain? Cooke City being beyond its boundaries an' all.'

The officer grunted. 'These murders took place on my post, and Turner was one of *my* men, all of which is enough for me. I intend sending a telegraph to the

Secretary of the Interior reporting all of this, but not until your pursuit party has left. Just in case he views things differently.'

'Fair enough, Captain,' Deke replied softly. Being an independent-minded civilian only employed by the army, he didn't shirk from having his say. 'I guess I was just asking the question, is all. Because you'll be responsible for anything that we get up to out there, and I ain't known for my patience!'

TO: SECRETARY OF THE INTERIOR LAMAR *STOP* FRANK POTTS — POACHER ARRESTED AND INCARCERATED *STOP* THEN MURDERED LAST NIGHT ALONG WITH ONE OF MY ENLISTED MEN *STOP* A NUMBER OF UNKNOWN MEN INVOLVED *STOP* IT IS MY INTENTION TO SEND A DETAIL IN PURSUIT *STOP* DO YOU CONCUR *STOP* CAPTAIN HARRIS —

MILITARY SUPERINTENDANT MAMMOTH *STOP*

★ ★ ★

'There's a problem.'

'So deal with it.'

The two men, both sporting long flowing beards and wearing elegant frockcoats, sat at a corner table in Mades' Restaurant on 3rd Street, Washington DC. In very opulent surroundings, the exclusively wealthy clientele were comfortably remote from the hustle and bustle, and the clatter of carriages outside. If the inclination took them, they might gaze out over the frog pond in the back yard where customers could, if they so wished, select their dinner while it still lived. Of course there were more than just frogs legs on the menu in this well-regarded German establishment, where the main attraction was actually the 'chicken dinner'. Sadly, such culinary delights would have to wait for a while for these two particular customers as they had more pressing matters to consider. A suitably deferential waiter had already been waved away after getting no further than the drinks order.

'It might not be anything like as simple as that,' replied the US Secretary of the Interior in notably hushed tones. He was a long-faced individual going by the improbable name of Lucius Quintus Cincinnatus Lamar. 'It seems as though that fool Lomax, or one of his cronies, has murdered an army-enlisted man in Mammoth, along with a hunter employed to shoot food for the surveyors.'

'Killing the man that's paid to feed them sounds a little cavalier,' remarked the other worthy, a well-known financier by the name of Jay Cooke. 'Did they eat *him* instead?'

Secretary Lamar snorted disparagingly. He really couldn't detect a humorous aspect to any of this. 'Captain Harris, the park superintendent, is a very diligent officer. He wants to seek redress for the killings, and such action could open up a whole can of worms. Considering what's at stake, I have to say you seem to be taking my news very calmly.'

Cooke, the older man by four years at sixty-six, suddenly regarded the cabinet member with the intense gaze of a striking snake. 'That's because all I stand to lose is money,' he retorted sibilantly. 'Such a thing has happened before, and I can get over it. Don't forget, my bankruptcy nearly brought the country to its knees in '73, for God's sake, and now look at me: dining with the highest in the land. You, on the other hand, could find yourself not only out of government but also in a federal penitentiary. Think about that while you're gnawing on a frog's leg!'

TO CAPTAIN HARRIS *STOP* DISTRESSED BY YOUR CASUALTY *STOP* NEVERTHELESS UNDER NO CIRCUMSTANCES MUST THERE BE ANY PURSUIT *STOP* THE ARMY HAS NO JUSIDICTION IN COOKE CITY

41

STOP I WILL NOTIFY RELE-
VANT CIVILIAN AUTHORITIES
STOP IT IS FOR THEM TO
APPREHEND THE KILL-
ERS *STOP* ACKNOWLEDGE
RECEIPT OF AND UNDER-
STANDING OF THIS MESSAGE
STOP SECRETARY OF THE
INTERIOR LAMAR *STOP*

* * *

Later the same afternoon, in far less salubrious surroundings, Moses Harris stared long and hard at the reply to his telegram. The light was beginning to drain from the wintry sky, and he had already got a kerosene lamp burning in his sparse office. The artificial light source also provided a welcome semblance of heat that, when combined with the hot stove in the corner, kept the temperature tolerable . . . until inevitably somebody would open the god-damned door!

The captain was attempting to fathom out just what was so unsatisfactory about his exalted superior's response . . . other than the instructions, of course. Then it came to him. *His* telegram had made no mention of Cooke City. Secretary Lamar, although nominally a Civil War veteran with the losing side, hadn't been west of the Mississippi. So how did he know where the fugitives were likely heading? There was any number of towns to the north of Yellowstone, along the route of the Northern Pacific Railroad, which were far more likely to have been their destination.

All of a sudden, the career soldier detected a rotten stench of corruption in the air. It was no secret that many government officials had lined their own pockets in the recent past, and doubtless the practice was still prevalent. That was one reason why Commanding General Phil Sheridan, a strong supporter of Yellowstone, had got his way in sending the army in to patrol the national park. All of which made Harris wonder just what Allard's detail might be getting themselves into. He swore bitterly. It was too late to warn them now. The five men had been gone for hours, and there was no direct telegraph connection between Mammoth and Cooke City. And even if there had been, he wouldn't have known whom to contact. The mining camp, surrounded by the park, but not actually in it, was an unknown quantity to the US Army. Harris just wished he'd been able to send more men, but the fifty members of Company M were tasked with patrolling thousands of square miles, and small squads of them, each under a non-com, were out there doing just that. No, all the officer could do was trust to Allard and Wilson's competence and hope for the best. He knew a little of the latter's chequered past, and was glad that such a man had gone along. The pursuit party might well need all the help it could get!

★ ★ ★

The crash of a rifle discharging brought the five men to an abrupt halt. It was close to their position. Real close.

Instinctively, the four soldiers glanced at their scout for an opinion. That man didn't even have to think about it.

'Some kind of buffalo gun. Very probably a Remington .50-70.'

'How the hell's he know that?' muttered Private Tyler, but nobody was really listening to him. His sergeant in particular had a far more relevant question.

'The light's nearly gone. Ain't it a bit late in the day for someone to be hunting?'

Deke Wilson shook his head emphatically. 'Not if you're a poacher. A kill's a kill, and he'll know the park's patrolled by you blue bellies. If he was to get unlucky, then he might could be able to use the darkness to get away.'

'God damn it!' Charlie Allard exclaimed. 'We ain't got time for this. There's bigger fish to fry.'

The pursuit party had spent the long hours since leaving Mammoth skiing hard and fast directly eastwards. Both the army post and their destination, Cooke

City, were at similar latitudes, but there was a hell of a lot of snow-covered terrain in between. Although tired and sweaty, the men were keen to keep moving until the last of the light had gone, because all of them had seen the sickening condition of Lane Turner after his killer had finished with him. The sight was etched in their brains, and each of them had it in mind to set things aright. And yet, in spite of all that, there was just no escaping the main reason for their presence in Yellowstone.

'Are we on park land or off it?' the non-com queried reluctantly. In his mid-thirties, he was older than the other soldiers, and recognized that the stripes on the sleeves of his tunic brought responsibilities as well as greater pay.

Wilson pondered for a moment. 'My money would be on it, but I'll tell the captain anything you want me to.'

Allard grunted. 'It's nearly time to make camp. Let's see if we can't invite a guest or two for supper.'

The scout shrugged. 'It's your call!'

After replacing the spent cartridge, Van Dyke closed the breech on his Remington Rolling Block Rifle and then lowered the hammer carefully. One bullet had been sufficient to finish the lone buffalo. Its great hairy bulk lay unmoving some fifty yards away. Fresh blood stained a patch of snow next to it. The luckless beast had spotted him in plenty of time but, as usual in winter, had been unable to escape through the deep drift. For the first time since leaving Cooke City, the lean-faced poacher had something to smile about. Turning back to his companion, he remarked, 'Seems like that damn sled is finally gonna earn its keep, Tom.'

'If I've told you once, I've told you a thousand times,' the other man retorted sourly. 'It's Thomas, *not* Tom!' Nevertheless, there was a certain spring to his movements as he began to drag the sled over. A long cord leading from it was fastened around his waist so that he had his

47

hands free to work the single pole.

Van Dyke opened his mouth to respond, but it froze in mid-action as he suddenly discovered to his dismay that the park was disagreeably overly crowded for the time of year. Four widely spaced figures on skis were moving rapidly towards the poachers and their kill. Reacting instinctively, he cocked his Remington, but held back from actually aiming it.

Seeing the startled expression, Thomas Garfield slid to a stop and swung around. 'Oh, shit,' was the best that he could manage. Then he let go of the pole and reached for his own Remington.

'United States Army. You're under arrest,' Allard bellowed out, as he and the three enlisted men swept closer. They were on a downward slope, and the going was easy. The poachers and their prey were in a sheltered dip in the landscape. As before with Frank Potts, the sergeant had the assurance of knowing that Deke Wilson was back there with his 'big fifty', but he really didn't want any gunplay. 'Drop those long guns now, or it'll go badly for you.'

Garfield and Van Dyke both had their Remingtons to hand, and neither felt inclined to just discard them meekly. They were hard-bitten, self-reliant individuals who didn't take kindly to authority of any sort. As the four soldiers came to a halt before them, the two men glanced meaningfully at each other and nodded. It was Van Dyke who had the words.

'Don't get uppity, soldier boy. We're here on private business, so you go on about yours an' we won't say anymore about this.'

Allard shook his head slowly. 'Believe me, I'd like to do just that. But the army gave me my stripes because I'm a good soldier, an' there ain't no private hunting allowed in Yellowstone. So I'll say it again. Drop them guns now!' Even as he spoke, the non-com swung the carbine from his shoulder. As his men copied him, Garfield thumbed back the hammer on his Remington.

Both poachers now had cocked rifles

pointing vaguely between the ground and the newcomers, whereas the military merely held theirs in a distinctly non-threatening manner. Again, it was Van Dyke who was the apparent push-hard. 'I've heard me a few stories about them Trapdoor Springfields you're all toting,' he crowed with obvious relish. 'Some say the actions get stiff, or even freeze up in really cold weather, kinda like we've got now. An' lookee here: you fellas ain't even cocked any of them yet. Now these Remingtons are something else entirely. They're a real peach of a gun. I reckon we could drop all four of you before you even got a shot off. What do you say to that?'

Allard sighed. He seemed to have been doing quite a bit of that lately. He knew that there was a fair bit of truth to what the hunter had just said. Although the sergeant and his visible men outnumbered them two to one, he had no desire to take any casualties. It was time to play his hidden ace.

'I ain't gainsaying any of what you've

just said. Only thing is we're not alone. There's a Sharps somewhere back in the snow behind us, with a two and a half inch cartridge in it that could put you down even if you were stood in New York City. So just do us all a favour and lay those damn guns in the snow.'

As Van Dyke stared intently at the soldier, a tiny dagger began to work in his guts. It was entirely possible that the other man was lying, but conversely there had been an undeniable ring of authenticity to his words. Then again, he and his partner had put an awful lot of effort into finding and killing that buffalo. 'Oh, the hell with it,' he muttered, and raised his rifle.

* * *

'Damn!'

Deke Wilson uttered the mild expletive with a great deal of passion. Contrary to some folks' way of thinking, he didn't actually enjoy killing. Yet there were times when it just couldn't be avoided.

This was one of them. In failing light, both targets were too far away for him to take a chance on merely wounding, because he had four young soldiers depending on him. Such considerations were processed in the time it took him to instinctively draw a bead on the man who was about to die.

As the poacher nearest the dead prey levelled his Remington, Wilson held his breath and squeezed the second trigger. There was a tremendous roar, and as his shoulder absorbed the punishing recoil, a great cloud of acrid smoke effectively gave away the marksman's position. Without troubling to check the fall of shot, he rolled three times to his right through the powdery snow, and then levered down the breech-block to reload. He knew without any doubt that only the one poacher remained alive, and if he had to kill him too, he would do so.

★ ★ ★

The .50 calibre bullet struck Van Dyke squarely in his chest, flattened out some inside of him, and then exited his back in an explosion of blood and gore. With an exquisitely vindictive twist, the misshapen lump of lead finally ended up inside the poor creature that he had just slaughtered. His abruptly lifeless body toppled backwards. The fact that his feet were still strapped to the long skis ensured that it came to rest at a distinctly bizarre angle.

Even though they had expected some form of violent action from their concealed scout, none of the three young privates had previously witnessed the devastating effect of such a powerful rifle. Their eyes widened in surprise, but it was nothing to Thomas Garfield's reaction. Horrified, his mouth fell open like that of a slack-jawed yokel, and he dropped the Remington as though it was suddenly white hot.

'Jesus, you really kilt him!' he exclaimed. 'He was just funning. We wouldn't really have shot any of you boys.'

Allard shook his head despairingly. 'You stupid bastard. This ain't just some sort of game.' Turning briefly, he waved back towards Wilson's position. Then, glancing at the large sled, he added, 'That's just been confiscated, so it looks like we'll at least have us a nice fire tonight.'

* * *

By the time Deke Wilson rejoined them, the soldiers had searched Van Dyke's bloodied corpse and put Garfield to work slicing a few choice cuts off the buffalo. Their duty was to protect the animals, but since it was already dead by another's hand, their leader saw no reason why they all shouldn't feed well that night. Allard was now also the temporary owner of two Remington rifles, along with a pocket full of cartridges. Looking them over, he had no doubt that they would provide a good deal more stopping power than the army issue Springfield.

His hands dripping with blood, the

poacher gazed sourly over at the new arrival. 'What the hell did you use on my partner, a mountain howitzer?'

The scout viewed him coldly. 'He called it, mister. And from where I was watching, the sergeant here gave him a sight more chance than you gave that buffalo.'

Before Garfield could respond, Allard cut in. 'Enough talk for now. The light's nearly gone and we need to get a camp-fire going. We'll head back to the trees for some shelter. You, poacher: load those steaks onto your sled, pronto. Might as well get some use out of it afore it gets broken up and burnt. Then, after we've all eaten like kings, you an' me are gonna have a little chinwag.'

'What about him?' Garfield muttered, gesturing over at his former partner.

'Even wolves have got to eat,' the sergeant retorted unsympathetically, 'and I gave him every opportunity.'

It was Wilson who had the last word before they left. 'And be sure you cut the tongue out of that beast. It's years since

I had me one, and they've got to be the tastiest morsel I ever sunk my teeth into!'

★ ★ ★

The six men sat around the warming fire on waterproof sheets, five of them belching contentedly. Only Private Tyler seemed to be uncomfortably preoccupied, but his buddies were too busy anticipating the expected interrogation to notice. Beyond the cheery circle lay only endless snow and, for those without night vision, only inky blackness. Every one of them, even including the poacher, had gorged themselves on roasted buffalo meat. Allard had a sound reason for favouring Garfield with unwarranted good treatment. So much so that the man wasn't even in irons . . . yet. True to his word, Wilson had eagerly devoured most of the tongue, only sharing a portion of it with the non-com. It was only then, as they all sipped piping hot coffee from tin mugs, that the sergeant suddenly fixed his gaze on their prisoner.

'So tell me, mister, what's your name?'

Despite the circumstances of his captivity, that man was feeling relatively mellow . . . as had been intended. 'Garfield,' he responded readily. '*Thomas* Garfield. An' I don't take to it being shortened.'

'To what, *Field*?' queried Wilson drolly.

The poacher appeared genuinely puzzled. 'No. *Tom*, of course.'

'And what do you know of Frank Potts?' Allard continued, his eyes suddenly like gimlets.

Garfield wasn't an intelligent man by any means, but he did possess a certain native cunning. His eyes narrowed suspiciously as he replied with his own question. 'What's he to you?'

Surprisingly, the sergeant's face lit up in a bright smile. 'OK, OK, Thomas. I can see you're way too sharp for me. So I'm gonna level with you. Potts is dead. Murdered in the army post at Mammoth, apparently by the very men that employed him. *And* they butchered an enlisted man as well. So we want them real bad!' He scrutinised the other man closely for his reaction, and wasn't disappointed. Garfield couldn't hide his shock, but there was far more besides: an intriguing mixture of fear and relief, which wasn't missed by his sharp-eyed interrogator.

'It's obvious you know who he was working for,' Allard began again. 'And you're gonna tell me.'

The poacher had been caught off guard but, hardened by life, he soon recovered enough to resort to bartering. 'And what's in it for me?'

The soldier nodded understandingly. 'If you tell me, we'll turn you loose when we reach the park's limits, well before Cooke City. That way no one will connect you with us. But if you *don't* talk, we'll take you into town with us and spread the word around that you're now working as an informer for the army. Potts ended up with his throat cut out, and I reckon you'd turn up the same. So what'll it be?'

It didn't take Garfield long to reach

a decision. 'You sure don't cut a man much slack, do you? The boss is a tall cuss by the name of Ben Lomax. Short grey hair and kind of cocky-looking. Acts as though someone like me is just a bad smell under his nose. Hear tell he works for the Northern Pacific Railroad. He had four fellas toting boxes of measuring gear and poles. He wanted someone to hunt for them in the northeastern part of Yellowstone, between Cooke City and the railroad. The money was good, and I was interested, until I saw who else was working for him.'

Allard waited expectantly. Something told him that this sixth man would be the one they were really after.

'A real mean pus weasel called Tatum. He was hired on as a guide, but if you're looking for a killer, he's your man. An' I didn't want anything to do with him.'

Deke Wilson inhaled sharply, attracting the non-com's attention. 'You heard of this Tatum fella?'

The scout nodded slowly. 'Oh yeah. I've never actually met him, but it's said he's a killer all right. One of the worst, because he actually enjoys it.'

'And one more thing,' Garfield continued. It seemed as though, having been persuaded to talk, he just couldn't stop, and he wasn't intelligent enough to realize that what he was saying might affect the deal that had been struck. 'They were putting the word out for buffalo hunters, as though there was something special cooking. Only there was something odd about it: they weren't bothered about hides or heads, or even the meat. They just wanted kills. A bit like in the old days, when the army just wanted all the buffalo dead to leave the Sioux and other hostiles without food. But that's all different now . . . isn't it? You blue bellies have gone all soft on them big shaggies.'

'But you still weren't interested?' Allard pressed him.

The poacher shook his head. 'Van Dyke and I prefer to work as a team, collecting the heads for top dollar. Or we did do,' he added, glancing accusingly at Wilson. 'And that Tatum gave us the shits. Come to think on it, you've got a bit of the same look.' And with that, he fell silent, as though suddenly very conscious of having run off at the mouth.

The sergeant nodded thoughtfully. It occurred to him that they seemed to be getting into something far more than just the pursuit of some assassin, and he abruptly wished that the captain had come along. So much so that he decided there would have to be a change of plan. Nodding at the scout, he remarked, 'Get those irons on him, Deke. Just so he doesn't try to hightail it in the night.' Ignoring Garfield's outraged protests, he switched his attention to the three enlisted men. 'You all heard what this piece of shit just said. Come first light, you, Burns, and you, Price, are heading back to Mammoth, taking him along. We can't risk letting him loose near Cooke City when we're there, and in any case Captain Harris is gonna want to talk with him.' Glancing at the now almost apoplectic poacher, he remarked, 'Yeah, I lied. Put in a complaint.' Then it was

61

back to the two privates. 'Tell the captain everything you just heard, and tell him Sergeant Allard would greatly value his help. Savvy?'

The two privates nodded solemnly. They were both levelheaded men who could be trusted to carry out such a task.

'And what do you aim to be doing while we're gone, Sergeant?' the soldier called Burns asked.

It was Deke Wilson who answered that. 'Stirring up a shit storm, I reckon!'

4

The Fourth Day

Ben Lomax drew in a deep breath as he gazed around the shithole that was Cooke City. He had just passed an uncomfortable night in a foul-smelling flophouse, which was the nearest thing to a hotel that the place possessed. Not for the first time, it occurred to him that for someone who had little liking for the frontier, he seemed to spend an awful lot of time on it. Yet there could be no denying that there was some real money to be made out West, and if this particular scheme came to fruition, there might well be enough coming his way to set him up for life. If, so to speak, he could keep the damn train on the tracks!

The designation of 'city' for such a settlement was definitely a misnomer. A rough and ready mining camp on land seized from the Crow Indians, it had been formerly known as Shoo-Fly, until a

63

certain infamous financier by the name of Jay Cooke took a fancy to the place. No doubt attracted by the silver deposits, he had promised to invest in it, and more specifically connect it up to the Northern Pacific Railroad. Then everyone in town would surely get rich. In a burst of greed-inspired enthusiasm, the few hundred occupants had renamed their camp Cooke City.

Unfortunately, it then transpired that there was one big problem. The surrounding land formed part of Yellowstone National Park. So long as that remained the case, the mere sixty miles separating the now impressively titled Cooke City from the nearest railroad town of Livingston might just as well have been six thousand. If the silver deposits were to be truly exploited, something would have to change. And the United States Congress would need to be persuaded that such a change was beneficial to the nation, because only that governing body could sanction the dismemberment of the national park in order that rails could be laid.

Regrettably, *progress* of any kind on the frontier had usually entailed the spilling of blood, and this was again proving to be true. As though confirming that fact, the man Tatum came into view on the mud churned Main Street. The building that he'd just left was one of the many saloons-cum-whorehouses in the camp. On catching sight of his employer, he favoured Lomax with a sardonic smile before moving over to join him. Even in camp, he had his repeating rifle slung across his back.

'Kind of early to be in a saloon, isn't it?' Lomax possessed a crisp and authoritative tone, which usually commanded respect, but he was beginning to recognize that a man of Tatum's lethal ilk was completely indifferent to it.

'Didn't seem that way last night. And once I got in the place, well, there was no good reason to leave. Besides, I've found you some more horse killers.'

Lomax couldn't hide his confusion. 'Horse killers?'

Tatum sighed and stepped forward, until they were quite literally nose-to-nose. The reek of cheap red eye was almost overpowering. 'Surely you don't want me telling everyone what you're really up to. Do you, *Mister Lomax*?'

The railroad man recoiled slightly. He wasn't used to being addressed in such a fashion. And yet, this uncouth gun thug had an edge to him that was quite chilling, coupled with an assassin's eyes that bored right into their target. It took a concerted effort to remind himself that the fellow actually worked for him, and that it was time to get the show on the road.

'You'd do well to recall that you're getting paid top dollar for all this,' he retorted, before moving on swiftly. 'I'm accompanying the surveyors on up to Livingston where we can compile our reports. I want you to take your men and head north, back into the park. Kill every buffalo you come across. What you do with the heads and hides is your business, but come the spring I don't want a single beast left alive between here and the railroad. If there's no buffalo up there, then there's no need for that chunk of land to remain part of Yellowstone.'

Tatum regarded his employer with mixed feelings, but nevertheless nodded his acceptance. He didn't like the arrogant railroad man one bit, but then again there were few men that he did take to. And there could be no denying that he was set to make one hell of a lot of money out of all this. The men that he had taken on to carry out the killing were happy to do it in exchange for outfitting, the term commonly used for providing ammunition and supplies. Their profit would come from the sale of body parts, leaving Tatum to keep all the money given to him by Lomax for their employment. All he had to do was keep the law off their backs. It really was a pretty sweet deal, except for maybe one little matter . . .

'And what if the army comes looking for a man killer? You gave the order, remember?'

Lomax paled slightly. He'd been trying

to put that incident out of his mind, and had largely succeeded. 'Me and my men will have left town, and I'd advise you and yours to do the same pronto. That way, if any soldiers do turn up here, they won't know who they're looking for anyway, and they'll just find a bunch of silver miners. I reckon most of them know who and what you are, so they're not likely to volunteer any information, are they?'

Tatum grunted. He couldn't hide a certain grudging admiration. 'You've got it all thought out, haven't you?'

'That's why I get hired for these sorts of jobs,' Lomax replied somewhat smugly as he turned to leave.

It was then that the other man brought him down to earth. 'Yeah, well, you ain't the only man on wages. Have you forgotten something?'

Lomax favoured him with a chill smile. This was the only time he really had any control over his assassin, and so it was only after a fairly lengthy theatrical pause that he finally retrieved a small but heavy leather pouch from a pocket and handed it over. It contained an inspiring mix of freshly minted gold Eagles and Double Eagles. Under normal circumstances, producing such a quantity of hard cash in camp was asking for trouble but, as he'd just said, all the miners knew Tatum for what he was.

'Count it if you wish, but then I'm leaving.'

The hired gun chuckled mirthlessly. He could tell by the weight that the coins were made of gold. 'No need. I trust you . . . up to a point. When do I see you again?'

Lomax was suddenly very impatient to be off. 'Report to me in Livingston when your job is done. *Au revoir*, Tatum.'

'What the hell did you just say?'

'Ask a whore. They all pretend to speak French.' And with that, the railroad man turned and walked away, chuckling to himself.

'An' happen you'd know, carriage trade,' the other man muttered venomously.

★ ★ ★

As the three men approached the mining camp later on that day, it was very noticeable that one of them had a problem. Heavily favouring his left foot, his speed through the snow had decreased, and his companions were flanking him protectively. Private Tyler heaved a great sigh of relief when they finally came to a halt in sight of the rough-cut timber buildings. Nevertheless, his understandable display was tempered by nervousness. He was well aware that Charlie Allard was angry with him, and with good reason.

'For Christ sake!' the non-com exclaimed for perhaps the third time. 'Why didn't you tell me earlier about your frostbite? You could have exchanged with Burns or Price and gone back to Mammoth. The post surgeon's used to dealing with such things, but God knows what they'll have in this place.'

Tyler nodded miserably. 'I'm real sorry, Sarge. But Lane was a buddy of mine, see. We enlisted together, back

70

east. Seeing him butchered like he was kind of got to me. Whoever did it has gotta pay an' I want to be there.'

'Happen you'll pay dear for that wish unless we get you some doctoring fast,' Deke opined. 'Which is kind of a nuisance, because your blue uniforms are a mite obvious. I'd been hoping to go in alone first and sniff around for a while, but I guess there just ain't any choice.'

Such an observation only compounded Tyler's misery, but there could be no help for it. They would have to go in together. Because if they didn't, he might never walk again!

★ ★ ★

Captain Moses Harris presented the unexpected arrivals with his usual calm demeanour, but beneath the surface he was seething. Private Burns had volunteered the words, and having listened patiently to his report it was obvious to the officer that his suspicions about Secretary Lamar had some basis. That belief was compounded by the fact that he had received a further telegraph from him demanding an acknowledgement of his first message. This one contained a noticeable edge of hysteria that only encouraged Harris to ignore it. There was quite obviously some very dark intrigue unfolding in Yellowstone Park, which so far encompassed two murders. And it was all taking place on Harris's watch. Therefore it was down to him to challenge it. He didn't include Deke Wilson's killing of Van Dyke in all of this. Unfortunate as that was, it only represented a case of resisting arrest.

'It's too late in the day to set out now, but come first light I'm making for Cooke City,' he announced suddenly. 'You two are good men, which is why I sent you with Sergeant Allard in the first place. So get a good night's rest, because you'll be coming with me. Now where's this damn poacher you've brought back?'

Private Price grinned wearily. 'He's chained to the hitching post outside, sir. He's not a happy man.'

Harris grunted dismissively and strode to the door of his office. The complaints began as soon as he opened it.

'I ain't some goddamned wild beast to be chained up,' Thomas Garfield bellowed. 'I told your poxy sergeant all he wanted to know and then some. So get these tarnal irons off of me now!'

The captain regarded him dispassionately. 'My men tell me that you did indeed cooperate with Sergeant Allard, so you will be released, but not until I return to the post. I might just need you as a witness. So until then, for your own safety, you're staying here. Think on all this next time you fancy shooting some poor dumb animal for profit.'

As though preparing to unleash a great torrent of invective, Garfield drew in a huge draught of freezing air, but what Harris said next stopped him in his tracks.

'If you say another word, I'll have you locked up in the same cell where Frank Potts had his throat cut out!'

The poacher's mouth shut like a trap.

73

'So what brings the army to Cooke City? A little off your range, ain't it?'

Charlie Allard and his two companions had just entered a singularly foul-smelling shack built next to the Miners' Saloon on Main Street. The sign above the door read: JED SAWYER. TOOTHS PULLED. LIMBS RESET.

'This young fella's in need of a sawbones,' Wilson announced, thrusting a reluctant Tyler towards their host. 'Touch of frostbite that's like to turn bad if it ain't already,' he added darkly.

A knowing smile creased the proprietor's grey features. He was a heavy-set individual of indeterminate age with greasy hair, and rotten teeth that were themselves in obvious need of pulling. Remnants of his last meal clung to his thick woollen sweater. There was nothing at all reassuring about such a man, but unfortunately he was the only person in town professing any medical knowledge.

'An' you got money to pay?' Sawyer

demanded brusquely.

'Yeah, we got money,' Allard retorted, already taking a dislike to the civilian.

'Well then, better get yourself on here, boy,' the sawbones remarked to Tyler with noticeable condescension. So saying, he swept the varied contents of a well-worn trestle table onto the floor casually.

The young soldier complied hesitantly. His foot hurt like hell, and he didn't feel well at all, but the prospect of actually seeing the damage was even less appealing. Once Tyler was on his back, Sawyer lost no time in removing his footwear, starting with the fur overboots.

'Whatever you got under there, this here's the cause, sonny,' he triumphantly announced, poking his finger through a hole in the side of the leather. The private yelled with pain, but Sawyer was unrepentant. 'Need to look after your feet better in these latitudes,' he continued. 'You can't tell me you didn't know these boots were getting wore out.'

The sight that greeted Tyler as his sock

was finally peeled back chilled him to the bone. He tried to swallow, but his mouth was suddenly just too dry. 'Oh, Jesus,' he croaked. The three smallest toes on his left foot had swollen horribly and turned partially black, so that he could hardly recognize them as his own. They were sticky with fluid that had seeped from various cracks in the skin. Somehow the warmth in the stove-heated room only seemed to have increased the pain. Out in the snow, and physically active, he had managed to live with it . . . just.

'Well that's simply dandy,' exclaimed his sergeant in disgust. 'Didn't they tell you in basic training that, next to your rifle, your feet are your most important piece of equipment?'

Temporarily overwhelmed by fear and misery, Tyler had nothing to say. He'd heard stories about the ghastly effects of gangrene on the body, and could only assume it was to be his fate as well.

'What can you do for him?' Allard demanded.

Sawyer's unpleasant features abruptly

76

registered pure avarice. 'He needs to stay with his foot raised above his head. His toes need greasing and keeping warm, and then all we can do is wait and see. It may end up that he needs to lose them to avoid greenrod setting in, and I can do that as well. But before I get to greasing anything, someone needs to grease my palm with silver, 'cause I ain't working for free.' With that, he reached out his right hand with the palm spread and waited.

The non-com stared at him long and hard, until finally he reached into a pocket of his blue tunic. With great reluctance, he produced five shiny silver dollars and dropped them into the other's hand.

'And then some,' Sawyer sneered. 'This here's a mining camp. Everything costs big bucks.'

Allard ground his teeth together, before parting with another five coins. 'I'm just an army sergeant, not some high roller. That's all you get until we see just how good you are.'

Sawyer grunted. 'OK, OK. No need to

get wrathy. Now give me some room, so's I can get to work.' With that, he retrieved a form of metal stirrup from a corner of the room. Placing it on the table, he then lifted Tyler's leg none too gently so that the ankle rested on it. Still in shock at the sight of his foot, the patient merely whimpered submissively.

Deke Wilson had deliberately kept out of the financial negotiations, because there were other things on his mind. This young soldier was a nice kid, but his condition was jeopardising the real reason that they were out there, and it was his own damn fault. So he waited until the slimy cockchafer of a sawbones was rather cavalierly applying some kind of grease to three very tender toes, before suddenly springing the question.

'Where's that son of a bitch Tatum right now?'

Jed Sawyer's face was a picture, and one that told Wilson everything that he needed to know. With his mind occupied by both the task at hand and the silver dollars in his pocket, the sawbones was ill prepared to fend off such an enquiry. Realizing that the hard-faced newcomer was watching him like a hawk, the best he could manage was to try and stall.

'Tatum? I think I've heard that name before.'

'Oh, you can do a whole lot better than that,' Wilson scoffed. 'An upstanding gent like you will know everything that's happening in a dump like this. We've brung you some doctoring business, so don't go spoiling it for yourself. Just tell me where he is an' I'll get out of your face.' With that, he tapped the muzzle of his Sharps on the table loudly.

Sawyer jumped, and so did his patient. Greasing temporarily forgotten, he stepped back from the table, and for the first time took a proper look at his interrogator. He quickly decided that he didn't like what he saw. There was something about the cold-eyed stranger with his big buffalo gun that set him on edge. He definitely wasn't just some run of the mill manure spreader like the other two. More like a killer for hire, akin to the man he was pursuing!

'He left this morning. Took some other fellas hunting.'

Wilson nodded, as though he had known it all along. 'An' let me guess. They all headed north into the park.'

The other man nodded silently. He'd already said far too much, and he suddenly wanted this mean-looking *hombre* out of his shack and out of his life.

The scout glanced meaningfully at Allard. 'Let's you and me take a look around.' Then to Sawyer, 'You look after this young fella like he was your kin, you hear? We'll be back.'

* * *

The two men stood on the rudimentary boardwalk, beside the ROOMS TO LET sign. By a remarkable coincidence, they were on exactly the same spot that Ben Lomax had occupied earlier that day. With darkness coming on they had secured a room for the night, but it was what happened afterwards that bothered the sergeant. 'I don't feel right happy, leaving Tyler all alone with that sticky fingered vulture. We could be gone for days.'

Deke Wilson shrugged. 'We've got a job to do, Charlie. We can't hang around in town waiting for his toes to drop off. There's a good chance we can catch up with this Tatum character, an' the captain should be along here in a day or two. If we leave word about Tyler here in the saloons and the hardware store, Harris should get the message.'

Very reluctantly, Charlie Allard nodded his head. 'I guess you've got the right of it, as usual, but I want Tyler out of that shack and in here before we leave. That way there's more than just Sawyer that gets to see him, 'cause I don't trust that greasy-looking son of a bitch!'

And so it was decided. They would leave at first light, and God help the sawbones if he messed up!

5

The Fifth Day

A fusillade of rifle shots crashed out in the sheltered valley, well to the north of Cooke City. After a wasted first day, the six men had suddenly struck pay dirt in the form of a small stand of buffalo. Not so many years past, fifty of the creatures would have been sniffed at, but now such numbers could be classed as a real find. Ten were already bleeding and down, felled by lead from a variety of firearms. The remainder were frantically trying to escape from the clearly visible hunters, but their massive weight in the deep snow meant that such efforts were likely to be futile.

In reality, only five of the men were firing. The sixth, with his Winchester at the ready, had no interest in the killing. Instead, he was relentlessly scrutinising their back trail, and the surrounding high ground. As an experienced hired gun,

Tatum didn't believe in 'out of sight, out of mind'. Apart from the slight chance of army patrols, the two murders in Mammoth were still recent, and could yet have consequences that he fully intended to be ready for. And then, of course, there was always the totally unexpected.

Another ragged burst of gunfire resulted in ten more animals either dead or dying. The white landscape was now liberally dotted with bright splashes of red, and one of the hunters yelled exultantly over to their taciturn sentinel, 'This is like shooting fish in a barrel!' Like the others, he was a disillusioned miner who had found work at the diggings far too hard for his tastes. It didn't matter that he was a mediocre shot at best, because there was little skill required. 'What the hell you watching out for, anyhu? There ain't another human being within thirty miles!'

Tatum's hard eyes settled on him briefly. 'That's what you reckon, huh?' Then he pointed over casually to a group of around a dozen mounted figures sitting their ponies some three hundred yards away. 'So who the hell are they? Elk, or maybe antelope?'

As the former silver miner peered off in the direction indicated his eyes widened like saucers. 'Oh, shit!' he muttered in abject horror. 'We're all going to be scalped. I've heard all about these Cheyenne Dog Soldiers!'

Tatum was aware that the firing had stopped as the others spotted the band of Indians, but he kept his attention where it mattered. 'You've been reading too many dime novels, fella. Them's Sioux, I reckon. Maybe just looking us over, or maybe not.'

'What do we do?' the other man wailed unhappily, now quite obviously wishing that he'd never left Cooke City.

The gunhand levered a cartridge into the breech of his Winchester slowly, a movement that also cocked the weapon. The Sioux, covered from neck to toe in animal furs, appeared to be armed with a mixture of bows and rifles. The question was, were they hostile or not?

'All of you aim your guns at them, but *don't* shoot, no matter what I do. Savvy?'

'But what *are* you gonna do?' pressed the anxious miner, even as his cronies did as ordered.

'Give them to understand our intentions is serious,' Tatum retorted, and suddenly his right hand was a blur of movement. He fired and then worked the under-lever five times in rapid succession, so that when he'd finished there was a bank of acrid smoke before him. Every bullet had been carefully targeted, but not a single brave had toppled from their ponies. Instead, three holes had appeared in the snow directly in front of them, and a tree on either side had been struck. The Sioux remained in place, as though nothing had happened, but they couldn't fail to have been impressed by the skilful display.

'Hot dang! That was some shooting, mister,' one of the hunters opined.

The others remained silent, nervously watching the Indians for any reaction. For long moments, those individuals

85

regarded the hated buffalo hunters with apparent indifference. Then, as one, the whole group merely turned their mounts away, and rode off slowly.

'Yeehah!' the last speaker bawled out. 'It looks like those mangy scavengers ain't got the stomach for mixing it with white folks anymore.'

Tatum regarded him scornfully. 'Don't ever take those red men for granted. In their day, you couldn't have held a candle to them.' Glancing around at the others, he added, 'Who told you sons of bitches to stop shooting, anyway? I want every one of those buffalo dead, along with any others we come across in this section of Yellowstone.'

As the men complied, it never occurred to any of them to wonder why their cold-eyed employer was so keen to have animals slaughtered when he had no interest in profiting from it. Tatum, having dealt with the unexpected, fed five fresh cartridges through the loading gate of his rifle, before picking up the empties methodically. Confident that no one was observing him, he suddenly displayed a broad smile. Out in the wild, he was surely in his element. As anyone would find out, if they should attempt to best him!

★ ★ ★

Having left Private Tyler in the dubious care of Jed Sawyer, the two men had spent the whole morning travelling fast and hard. Even on relatively flat virgin snow, the effort involved in poling the skis was prodigious. By the time the watery sun had reached its zenith, it was well past time to replenish their energy. Pemmican, both nutritious and delicious, was ideal. They contentedly scoffed the mixture of berries, fat and dried meat by the handful. Yet even then they always maintained a wary eye on their surroundings. The harsh, white-coated landscape was totally devoid of any apparent life. Ahead of them to the north, their obvious route was bordered by tree-covered high ground. That meant less snow, but was impractical for anyone travelling on skis.

'Goddamn, but this is fine stuff,' Allard opined between mouthfuls. 'I just never tire of it.'

Deke Wilson smiled, his jaws working strongly. Still hungry, he reached into his pouch . . . and froze rigid. Then, his food entirely forgotten, he tilted his head slightly and sniffed the air.

The sergeant knew better than to interrupt. Instead, he reached for the recently acquired Remington on his back. Although such a rifle was new to him, Wilson had left him in no doubt that it was superior to his regulation issue Springfield, and so that weapon had been left in Cooke City for collection later.

'Keep it pointing at the ground,' the scout, who never seemed to miss anything, commanded abruptly. Even as he spoke, a group of horsemen emerged from the pines. The fleet-footed ponies, taking advantage of the lighter snow, were obviously adept at wending their way through the trees.

'This is all we need,' the non-com replied nervously. He had encountered plenty of Indians in his time and had lived to tell the tale, but the two white men were heavily outnumbered and far from any back up.

'Get that bearskin open pronto,' Wilson rasped. 'That way they won't have any doubts about just what we are.'

Allard complied swiftly. Having unbuttoned the heavy coat, he held it wide open, so that the blue tunic underneath was plain for all to see. The uniform obviously made some kind of impression, because after a brief pause, two of the warriors detached themselves from the main group and urged their ponies out into the deeper snow. Progress was laborious but, as they drew closer, one of the Indians patted the area over his heart and then reached that hand out in greeting.

'Seems like they want to trade something other than lead,' Wilson remarked, the relief in his voice very obvious as he reciprocated.

The spokesmen reined their ponies in a few yards in front of the white men. There then followed a complex dialogue that Allard found impossible to follow. It consisted of a jumbled mix of Pidgin English, sign language and guttural Sioux. Since he couldn't make any meaningful contribution to it, the soldier had to content himself with merely observing. He decided that the two Indians, although swathed in furs, had to be the wrong side of middle age, whatever that was amongst savages. There was sadness to their still proud features that possibly reflected the passing of their race from greatness. And yet, something about them still commanded respect . . . and not a little fear.

As the conversation suddenly came to an abrupt end, Wilson slowly raised his right hand, reached into a pocket, and withdrew a slab of chewing tobacco. With his knife, he carefully sliced it into three parts. Nodding encouragingly, he handed two pieces over to the expectant warriors. They grunted appreciatively, before urging their animals around and away.

Allard carefully eased the hammer down on his unfamiliar Remington, and then waited impatiently for a few moments before demanding, 'What the hell was all that about?'

'Seems like we've got a group of poachers up ahead. Slaughtering every buffalo on sight, just like in the old days. And one of them handles his repeater like he was born to it. Those Sioux believe that the army, which means you, should stop them. They fought your kind in the past, but at least they could respect you. Buffalo hunters, on the other hand, are the lowest form of life, and they have given us their blessing to kill them all. Since they still like to think of this as their land, it looks like we're working for the Sioux now,' Wilson concluded wryly, before slipping a piece of tobacco between his teeth and chewing contentedly.

★ ★ ★

Jed Sawyer was no stranger to dark thoughts, and right now the self-proclaimed physician was having an abundance of them. The pesky demands of this snivelling whelp with his frost-bitten toes were beginning to seriously irritate him. Ten dollars was scant payment for house calls, which was how he perceived his visits to the local flophouse. Because of his condition, the youthful patient had been exclusively allocated a tiny upstairs room at the rear, which only just accommodated the well-used mattress. The grimy space was unheated and far from ideal, but at least Private Tyler was out of the elements.

As Sawyer again glanced at the two Springfield Carbines leaning in the corner of the room, a thoroughly unpleasant idea began to take shape. In the isolated mining camp, such weapons would undoubtedly fetch good money. And it was quite likely that the annoying bluecoat would have some coins in his tunic as a bonus. All the young man had to do was die without any suspicious circumstances. And bleeding to death during a necessary amputation would entirely fit the bill. He switched his attention to the blackened toes, and remarked sourly, 'I've agreed with myself that if those haven't improved any by tomorrow, they'll have to come off.'

Tyler's pain-filled eyes widened with horror. 'They're gonna get better. You just see. And you heard what Mister Wilson said. You've got to look after me properly, or answer to him when he gets back.'

'You pathetic little shit,' Sawyer scoffed, any pretence at sympathy abruptly gone. 'You really don't understand, do you? Nobody goes gunning for a man like Tatum and survives. The next time you'll be seeing your buddies is when you join 'em in hell. An' I ain't laying bets on who'll be there first. Ha ha ha!'

* * *

The severed head, swinging gently at the end of a rope, swam into vision through his drawtube spyglass, and Deke Wilson grunted. He'd seen such grisly sights many times before, but it was never pretty. The valuable trophies were too heavy to be transported across deep snow to so-called civilisation, so poachers hung them from tree branches until the spring thaw. Until then, the extreme cold would preserve them in reasonable condition.

* * *

With around fifty buffalo killed, the trees bordering the killing ground resembled a hangman's hollow. The perpetrators were still putting the finishing touches to their work, because killing the defenceless creatures had been the easy part. Gorily detaching the massive heads, and then carrying them dripping with blood over to the tree line had involved a great deal of effort . . . but not by all of those present.

Wilson, lying flat and keeping his lens away from any residual sunlight, scrutinized one man with particular interest. Obviously possessing a stocky build, even under his fur coat, he stood apart from the others as they went about their bloodsoaked endeavours. With a Winchester at the ready, the sentry appeared to never be still. Even as his eyes roamed the surrounding terrain, his body ducked and weaved as though he were already under fire. In the army scout's mind, there was no doubt whatsoever. This was their man!

One other thing was very apparent: since none of the creatures had had their hides removed, it meant that the hunters were very likely not professionals. They were just opportunists, looking for a quick buck, and with no stomach for the really messy and time-consuming task of skinning.

Having backed away and related his findings to the anxious non-com, Wilson added, 'This is your detail, an' your call, but I want my say before we make any kind of move against those cockchafers!'

Allard shook his head in disbelief.

'Now why would you go and say a thing like that? You know damn well I wouldn't have it any other way. Let's hear it.'

'Well, first off, there's a sight too many of them for us to pussyfoot about. None of that "You're under arrest" shit. We'll have to hit them hard and kill everyone we can. An' now's not a good time. They're moving in and out amongst the trees. All those that we don't get with the first volley will use them for cover. The other problem is that the most dangerous of them is the one we want alive, 'cause he's got the answers.'

The sergeant blew out of his mouth like a horse. 'So what *do* you suggest?'

Wilson's expression was bleak. 'We move on them just before first light. That Tatum fella is as twitchy as hell, but since they can't know that we're out here, we should be able to catch them by surprise.' He stopped, and peered closely at his companion as they lay in the snow. 'What do you think of my plan?'

Allard's honest features were troubled. 'Not too keen on all the killing, I guess. That's not what I joined the army for. So if we catch 'em asleep, we'll just knock them senseless, is all. Other than that, I like it.'

The scout knew all too well that going easy on their more numerous opponents could well get them killed, but he chose to hold his peace. As always, he would do what needed to be done and argue about it later. So instead, he merely turned away and began to crawl back to the low rise that overlooked the killing ground.

'What are you about?' the soldier queried.

'We're gonna need to keep tabs on those fellas until they make camp. And besides, there's a whole spread of dead animals over yonder. I want to see if those bastards have missed any buffalo tongues.'

6

The Sixth Day

The campfire, originally stacked high against the biting cold, still put out both heat and illumination in that last hour before what would pass as first light arrived. Shadows danced beguilingly in the surrounding trees. For the two men approaching on their bellies, it made spotting their intended victims a whole lot easier. The five hunters and their ramrod lay with booted feet to the fire, wrapped up in thick blankets and coats. Apart from an occasional crackle in the embers, all was quiet.

Charlie Allard clutched his Remington in both hands, his intention being to use it as a non-lethal club. Deke Wilson carried his large hunting knife by its blade. It was also apparently intended as a club, but that was purely a concession to the sergeant's finer feelings, because when the need arose, the scout was a killer through and through.

Allard, his heart thumping like an anvil strike, took a last look at the sleeping men and then glanced at his companion. The long night's wait was finally over. It was time. He nodded. Wilson winked encouragingly, and then carefully eased his body out of the snow. Even while doing so, he changed the hold on his knife, so that he was now gripping it in the way it had been designed for. Being up against greater numbers was the only justification that he needed. Barely making a sound, the two men closed in on their victims.

It was Wilson who struck first. Without the slightest hesitation, he crouched over one of the poachers, placed his left hand over the man's mouth and plunged his blade into an exposed throat. The geyser of blood that resulted didn't trouble Wilson in the least, but Allard caught sight of it in his peripheral vision and it sure as hell startled him. In the act of slamming the Remington's butt down on an unprotected forehead, the shockingly unexpected scene affected his aim just enough. The heavy blow became a glancing one. His victim awoke with a great howl of pain, and abruptly all surprise had gone.

The reaction was mixed. A figure that could only be Tatum exploded out of his blanket like a scalded cat, whilst the other three were far more groggy and bemused. A true professional, the gunhand had slept curled up with his rifle, but by sheer bad fortune it was now tangled in that same blanket. The few desperate seconds required to disentangle it gave Wilson the time to gauge his next move.

Knowing that he was going to need his rifle, the best way to dispose of the knife was into someone's flesh. Although greasy with blood, he yanked it out of the dead man's throat and hurled it with great force into the chest of one of the three disorientated poachers. Emitting an agonised scream, the unlucky recipient collapsed back to the ground, out of the fight permanently.

Allard, now finally accepting that extreme violence was unavoidable, aimed his rifle at another opponent and snapped off a shot. As the brilliant muzzle flash flared in the night, a high-powered bullet slammed into his target. The luckless fellow had just got onto his haunches, and the momentum at such point-blank range threw him back away from the fire. He lay helplessly on the ground, his body twitching in its death throes.

As the sergeant first retracted the hammer frantically and then the breechblock to reload, Tatum finally managed to level his Winchester. With a cartridge already in the firing chamber, all he had to do was cock it. Wilson, in the meantime, knowing that a revolver was far better for close work, had drawn and cocked his Colt Army. Who would be the first to fire was almost too close to call.

The army scout just made it, and yet such was the pressure on him that he didn't have time for any deliberation. As the weapon emitted a reassuring crash, Tatum twisted sideways under the impact of a .45 calibre bullet. At the same time, his trigger finger contracted, and his rifle blasted its own load harmlessly off into the still dark sky. He had been hit in the right arm. How badly he didn't yet know.

As Wilson again cocked his piece for another try, his partner had managed to reload his Remington. Instinctively, he aimed at the only opponent still untouched, forgetting that he hadn't properly accounted for his first victim. That man, although he had blood streaming from a bad gash on his forehead, had reached for the nearest weapon to hand: a skinning knife. Peering unsteadily up at his assailant, he stabbed upwards impulsively. The wickedly sharp blade pierced Allard's groin and kept on going.

Releasing the high-pitched scream of a woman, the sergeant toppled backwards. Although hitting the hard ground with tremendous force, he desperately attempted to pull clear of the cold steel that so tormented him. Tenaciously, his intended prey kept after him, viciously twisting the long blade. Waves of unbearable agony swept over the non-com.

Deke Wilson suddenly had an unenviable number of choices: take a more considered, disabling shot at Tatum; shoot the unhurt poacher stone dead; or go to the aid of his companion. For once, hard logic gave way to sentiment. Swiftly drawing a bead on the knifeman, he fired two times in rapid succession. That man jerked twice under the lethal impacts and then lay still. His blood mingled with that of Allard's in the trampled snow. That man gave out another agonised scream, as he finally managed to crawl off the knife that was now so tightly held in a death grip.

By the time Wilson swung back to cover the two survivors, both of them had bolted, leaving all their belongings including precious skis by the fire. The only people remaining around it were now either dead or dying. 'God damn it all to hell,' he exclaimed. 'That didn't pan out!'

In an unpleasant reversal, it was now

he and Charlie that were illuminated by the campfire, whilst out in the trees there was at least one very dangerous man on the loose. On the point of dragging one of the corpses onto the embers to smother them, the scout abruptly thought better of it. Once daylight arrived, he would have plenty of things to be burnt. But until then, they would need to retreat from its circle, and quickly.

Moving swiftly over to his whimpering companion, Wilson remarked, 'I'm real sorry about this.' Then he seized Allard's wrists and dragged him now screaming across the snow, until they were clear of the firelight. Their route was marked by a wide trail of blood, and a cursory examination of the appalling wound revealed the sad truth.

'I can't do nothing for you, Charlie,' he muttered apologetically. 'Except maybe try to keep you warm.' So saying, he dashed back to the fire and seized a couple of blankets.

The sergeant stared at him through pain-filled eyes as the thick woollen covers were gently laid over him. It felt as though his insides had been carved out, and yet, mercifully, heavy blood loss meant that his agony was beginning to diminish. 'Why me?' he managed.

Wilson shook his head sadly. 'This ain't some kind of game between gentlemen. The old days ain't gone yet. It's still 'kill or be killed'. It's just a mortal shame you've learnt that too late.'

The non-com's eyes drifted for a moment. Then he suddenly gripped the other man's arm hard. Very hard. 'You got any buffalo tongue left?'

Wilson shook his head regretfully.

'That's what I figured,' Charlie Allard muttered almost inaudibly, and then his head lolled back and he was gone.

'Damn, damn, damn,' the army scout exclaimed with great and genuine sadness.

* * *

'What's your given name, boy?'

Private Tyler peered vaguely up at

Jed Sawyer's thoroughly disagreeable features. The drab, pokey room was unheated, so he was literally numb with cold. Consequently, it actually took him a few moments to remember something so basic. 'Henry,' he finally replied.

Sawyer nodded portentously, as though the response in some way explained everything. 'Hmmm. Is that a fact? Well, Henry, it looks like you're caught between the sap and the bark.' He was carrying a grubby carpetbag, and there was a strange glint in his eyes as he continued. 'Them toes don't look any better to me, so the thing is, I'm gonna have to carry out a procedure that'll likely save your life . . . *if* you survive it! Problem is, *if* you do you'll never walk properly again. Happen it's a small price to pay, though. And as I just said, you *are* betwixt the sap and the bark. *Sap and bark*,' he repeated with even greater emphasis.

Then, as a now terrified Henry Tyler stared fixedly up at him, the surely unhinged sawbones opened his bag and produced a viciously serrated bone saw. 'You'll thank me for this, one day, but I gotta tell you, it will hurt,' he added with a theatrical flourish. For some sick reason, he had decided to maintain the fiction that his patient was actually going to survive the treatment.

The young soldier, frightened out of his wits and all alone in a strange town, made to rise up from the mattress. 'You ain't coming anywhere near me with that cutting tool, mister!' he yelled hysterically. Then he began to shout for help. Sadly, he could never have anticipated Sawyer's next action.

Moving with astonishing speed, that man's hand again dipped into his bag, and this time came out holding a wooden mallet. Like a striking snake, Sawyer swung it at his patient's forehead. It connected with a tremendous thwack, knocking Tyler senseless. 'Ha, works every time,' he chuckled manically. Perversely, with neither laudanum nor ether available in town, he had done the young man a favour.

Then, knowing full well that there wouldn't be any interruptions from the owner of the flophouse with whom he had an arrangement, the sometime surgeon moved around to the end of the mattress and knelt down next to the carbines that would soon be his. Exchanging the mallet for the bone saw, he placed the blade next to the badly swollen and no doubt exquisitely tender toes. Then the humorous side to the whole business began to tickle him, and the chuckles expanded into full-blown laughter. A man's life was cheap indeed out on the frontier!

★ ★ ★

Fighting a strong urge to move, Deke Wilson had remained low, next to Allard's corpse, until the new day had fully arrived. Only then did he retrieve his knife from his victim's bloodied chest and carry out a sweep of his surroundings after that, searching for sign. They were soon discovered, and told a predictable tale. Two sets of footprints had fled into the trees, accompanied by drops of blood. Tatum had then presumably bound his wound, before he doubled back to the camp, doubtless hoping to catch his remaining attacker unawares and illuminated by the fire. When that didn't work, he then returned to his waiting companion and together they had plodded off towards the north through deep snow.

Wilson poled his skis back to the lifeless encampment, all the while deep in thought. This Tatum knew his business. It was often the case that a wild animal was most dangerous when wounded, and so it might also be with this particular human. The army scout knew that he could soon overhaul them on skis, but did he really want to? Such a course would be fraught with risk. Far better to try and second guess the fugitives, and wait for them to arrive at their destination having got there first. The question was where might that be?

Four bloodied cadavers awaited him around the still warm fire, along with their meagre possessions. It seemed a great shame to burn the handcrafted skis, but there could be no avoiding it. He couldn't risk allowing the two survivors the opportunity to recover them in the unlikely event that they returned again. Reluctantly, he heaved them all onto the still hot embers. It took some time before they were engulfed in flames, but then he just couldn't resist luxuriating in the welcome heat that they produced.

In front of a now roaring fire, Wilson cleaned his bloodstained knife on one of his victims' trousers. Then he checked all their pockets. The take was predictable, and reflected their status as frontier low-lives. A few coins, some chewing tobacco and a couple of pouches of pemmican was the sum total, but all appreciated none-theless. There was a mixed selection of weaponry, but he couldn't burden him-self with all the extra weight. As it was, he did intend taking Allard's Remington, because that was just too good a gun to leave behind. The other firearms would be a windfall for any human scavengers that might chance upon the campsite. Unless, of course, they were Indians, and then superstition might well keep them clear of the bloody ground.

What he did do was recover as much compatible ammunition as possible, and his pockets were soon stuffed. He had already figured out what to do with some of the cartridges that were of no use to him. In the snow, between Sergeant Allard's blood-soaked corpse and the fire, Wilson utilized the brass cases to spell out one word in large letters. **LIVINGSTON**.

It was to be hoped that, if Captain Harris were following on, the cartridges would still be visible. Even if it snowed, there would probably be enough heat remaining from the skis to melt it. With that done, there was nothing else to keep him there. As the message demonstrated, Wilson had concluded that Tatum would be heading north for the railroad town, because his gut feeling indicated that the Northern Pacific Railroad was, albeit unwittingly, somehow involved in all this skulduggery.

On the point of skiing away, the army scout took a last long look at Sergeant Charlie Allard, Company M, 1st Cavalry. Had conditions permitted, he would willingly have buried him, but as it was he knew that the non-com would have understood. It was sufficient that Deke Wilson fully intended to avenge his death!

★ ★ ★

There were no warning footsteps on the rickety stairs, or even a civil knock announcing a desire to enter. Not that Sawyer would have heard, laughing loudly as he was. Instead, the door crashed open and a tall figure entered.

'What the hell's all this, then?' demanded Captain Moses Harris. The sight that greeted his eyes was the stuff that nightmares were made of. In the cold, tiny, foul-smelling room, one of his enlisted men lay prone on a mattress. Displaying a great lump on his forehead, the young man appeared to be barely conscious. Over by his feet, a disgusting looking varmint brandishing a bone saw appeared to be on the point of removing some toes. All in all, it was not what he had expected!

The doctor's manic laughter froze in his throat, but to his credit he recovered quickly. 'What's the meaning of this intrusion?' he blustered. 'Can't you see I've important work to do here?' And with that, he levelled the serrated blade next to the little toe again.

Harris responded with two specific actions. With his left hand he opened his thick coat, thereby displaying the blue tunic beneath. And his right hand suddenly held a Colt revolver, cocked and aimed. 'This man is under my command. Put that god-damned saw down now, or it will surely go badly for you!'

As he took in both the uniform and the gun, Sawyer blinked owlishly. With the prospect of both profit and entertainment dissipating, he lowered his surgical tool very reluctantly.

The captain nodded. 'Now get over here pronto. You've got some explaining to do . . . downstairs.'

Unfortunately, such was the lack of space that Harris had to turn sideways so as to allow Sawyer to get past. And that man was a tricky and devious individual. The bone saw now laid in plain sight, but not so the lump hammer. The handle of that nestled nicely in the palm of his hand. As he got within range, he suddenly attempted an awkward left-handed swing at the soldier's head. It was then that he discovered he wasn't dealing with an injured youngster. Harris blocked the blow instinctively with his right arm, and then smashed the barrel of his Colt into the side of Sawyer's head. That man groaned with pain, stumbled to the side, and promptly fell headlong down the steep flight of stairs. He landed at the bottom with a great thump, much to the surprise of Privates Burns and Price.

'Put that man in irons until I decide what's to be done with him,' Harris ordered.

'Not a lot of point, sir,' Burns replied. 'Neck's broke.'

'Huh, well, happen he deserved it,' the captain responded dismissively. 'Shift him out of the way and then get up here. Both of you.' Holstering his weapon, he then turned and knelt down next to Henry Tyler.

That young man had recovered some of his senses, and was now gazing with tremendous relief at his commanding officer. 'I'm powerful glad to see you, sir,' he managed.

'What are you doing in this shithole, private?' Harris demanded. 'What was Sergeant Allard thinking of?'

Tyler shrugged, but instantly regretted it as his head throbbed violently. 'I guess he just had a lot on his mind, sir,' he began haltingly, and then related the course of events slowly, up to Allard and Wilson's departure from Cooke City. By the time he finished, the room had grown excessively crowded, what with two more enlisted men packed inside. 'I sure do hope they catch up with the bastard that killed Lane.' With that, he fell silent and gazed expectantly up at his captain. He wasn't to be disappointed, because the officer soon came to a decision.

'Right. We're getting you into someplace with a stove. Burns will stay with you until you're fit to return to Mammoth with him. We don't want any more maniacs trying to saw your toes off. I've seen plenty of frostbite cases, and I reckon you'll make out just fine. Price, you're coming with me. We've got a trail to follow, and it sounds like the sergeant and Wilson may well need our help.'

It was a sad and cruel fact that, by then, Charlie Allard was already beyond all possible help!

* * *

There was an anger burning deep within Tatum that made him very dangerous company. The flesh wound to his right arm hurt like hell, but that was nothing to the indignation that he felt. Whoever had jumped them in the night had been good at their job, but that was no consolation. He was supposed to be better!

'What if that son of a bitch is after us right now?' whined the sole remaining buffalo hunter as he glanced back into the beautiful desolation behind them. 'With him on skis, an' all, he could be anywhere. Hell, he might even be drawing a bead on us right now.'

Tatum glanced at him dismissively. 'Nah. I've got a feeling about this one. He'll know we're watching out for him now. I reckon he'll try and second guess us, and head straight to where we're going. The thing is, he shouldn't know where we're going . . . unless someone's talked.'

Something in his tone made the poacher gaze at him nervously. 'Well, it sure weren't me. I ain't even met with the fella. Apart from when he tried to kill us, that is. Ha-ha.'

'Yeah, yeah,' Tatum muttered bleakly. He didn't take easily to company, and this moron was definitely beginning to irritate him.

For some time, the two men plodded along through the snow. Where possible, they kept to higher ground where it wasn't so deep. And so it was that, as they crested a small rise, they suddenly chanced upon a group of half a dozen buffalo in the middle distance. The massive creatures hadn't yet perceived the threat. It was a perfect opportunity to dispatch a few more of them. And yet the hunter from Cooke City seemed in no all fired hurry to start putting them down.

'What the hell are you waiting for?' Tatum demanded testily. His arm was aching something terrible and his whole demeanour reeked of menace. 'Them shells I gave you weren't just for target practice!'

The other man stared at him in disbelief. 'But if I start shooting, it'll give away our position for sure. And *he* might be out there!'

The gun thug sneered at him. 'You're

here to kill buffalo, so get to it.'

His employee shook his head emphatically. 'No way, mister. You might have some kind of death wish, but I ain't.'

A strange and very unsettling light suddenly seemed to glisten in Tatum's hard eyes as his left hand dropped into a pocket of his bearskin. 'Oh, I'm wishing for a death, all right, but it ain't mine.'

The other man jerked abruptly with shock, as a length of very cold steel penetrated his belly. Then, as the knife began to twist remorselessly in his guts, he let rip with a ghastly, inhuman scream, which effectively put the buffalo on notice that they were no longer alone. They began to scramble for safety, but of course the thick snow meant that they had scant chance of achieving that.

'Looks like I'll just have to shoot them myself,' Tatum remarked casually as he finally withdrew the blade. Ashen faced, and with blood now trickling from his mouth, his victim collapsed into the snow and lay twitching uncontrollably.

It suddenly occurred to Ben Lomax's

hired gun that he didn't even know the name of the man he'd first of all employed and then killed very casually. Something about that suddenly appealed to him enormously, and for the first time in ages he began to laugh uproariously. Then he cocked his Winchester and took aim at the nearest struggling creature. He had a long walk ahead of him to Livingston, so he might as well have a bit more fun first. And, if nothing else, he would at least come out of this with some delicious buffalo tongues!

7

The Seventh Day

One thing, above all else, placed Livingston far higher than Cooke City in the municipal pecking order. Having being instrumental in its creation, the Northern Pacific Railroad literally ran right through it, bringing guaranteed prosperity and high land values. In fact, the so-called city had even been named after one of that company's directors, a certain Johnston Livingston. And it wasn't just *any* railroad town either. Situated next to the Yellowstone River, it boasted massive engine sheds and workshops, where trains heading west could be serviced before ascending to the Bozeman Pass, which just happened to be the highest point on the whole line. With the benefit of a telegraph connection, it therefore made sound sense for Ben Lomax to use Livingston as his base. And his status as chief surveyor for the Northern Pacific ensured that he had the use of his own log cabin on the outskirts of town.

That afternoon, basking in the warmth from the iron stove whilst working on an exceptionally important report for one Jay Cooke, he just happened to glance through the single small window. What he saw was both intriguing and unsettling. A lone figure was skiing into town from the south, and more particularly *out* of Yellowstone Park. Lomax stared at him pensively. The fact that he didn't recognize him was of no comfort to a guilty mind. What business might one individual have in the park in the middle of winter?

The possession of *two* rifles slung over his shoulders marked him out as a poacher, but not one of Tatum's temporary employees. In their heyday, professional buffalo hunters out on the plains often utilised more than one high-powered gun, so as to avoid the barrels overheating when in continuous use. Yet the weather was freezing, and animal numbers minute, although not yet sufficiently so for Lomax's purposes. Then he noticed a particular detail that chilled him to the bone, as though the stove had abruptly ceased to exist. There was what looked like dried blood on the sleeves of the man's massive coat. One thing was for sure. The new arrival had definitely been killing something! And with Tatum's hunting party out there, certain questions required answers, because the surveyor had no liking for either insecurity or loose ends.

Spotting this fellow in the first place had been pure happenstance, but Lomax now decided that he had to keep him in sight, at least until he found out just who he was and what had brought him to Livingston. Grabbing his coat, he wrapped up against the bitter cold and headed for the door.

* * *

Deke Wilson had heard his destination long before he saw it. The unmistakeable sound of a steam whistle was like nothing else on earth, and yet was strangely comforting. Because it signified that, after a gruelling bout of cross-country skiing, he had finally reached the railroad town. Now, as if to confirm that fact, there was even a Minnetonka Class engine manoeuvring into a shed on the eastern edge of it.

Somehow, Livingston seemed the complete antithesis of Cooke City. Open and spacious, and ringed by snow-covered hills, it existed as a conduit for the two most modern types of transportation and communication. Sure, there was doubtless greed aplenty, but it all seemed somehow less grubby and primeval than the silver mining that went on in Cooke City. That was how the army scout perceived it, anyway, but then this was only his second visit to the place.

Reaching the tracks, Wilson slid to a halt and removed his skis for the first time that day. Knowing that it wasn't humanly possible for the two fugitives to have reached town or even anywhere near it, he therefore decided that he had time to attend to a pressing need, and Frank White's saloon would surely satisfy it.

Reaching the garishly painted single-storey building, he leaned his skis and pole against the wall and barged open a heavy door that was very likely permanently closed against the cold. The warm fug, which included tobacco smoke and various body odours, took him pleasantly by surprise. For a long moment he just stood there scrutinizing the clientele until a voice bellowed out, 'Shut the goddamn door, friend, if'en you're staying. These limp-dicked *hombres* ain't used to cold weather.'

As raucous laughter swelled around the room, Wilson smiled tolerantly and complied. Then, approaching the bar, he swung the two rifles from his shoulders gratefully and placed them up against it. The bartender, a black-haired heavyset individual, glanced at them before peering at him speculatively.

'You're sure loaded for bear, friend. What brings you to Livingston in such

God awful weather?'

'Good sipping whiskey,' Wilson replied studiedly. It had been well over a year since he had last frequented White's Saloon. That time it had been summer, and he'd been in the company of a couple of Harris's troopers, so it was very unlikely that anyone, including the bartender, would remember him. Then again, it often behoved people in such occupations to possess good memories. They lived longer that way!

'Ain't I seen you somewhere before?' the other man persisted, making no move to provide a drink.

'I doubt it,' Wilson answered amiably enough. 'Hell, without a shave and a bath, I couldn't rightly recognize myself.' Then, with just a hint of impatience, he tapped the bar top. 'Whiskey.'

'Sure, sure,' the other man responded, reaching for a bottle. 'You'll like this. We get cases of it shipped out here from the east. We can do that, being as how this place is next to a railroad. It ain't cheap, but something tells me you're good for it.' So saying, he poured two fingers of Buffalo Trace Whiskey into a shot glass, and waited expectantly for Wilson's reaction.

As he took a sip, the army scout's eyes widened expressively. 'Hot dang! Your ma didn't raise a liar,' he exclaimed. 'Now that's what I call a drink.'

'Only the best at Frank White's,' the bartender proclaimed loudly, for all the world acting as though he was the owner. At that moment, the front door opened and closed quickly against the weather. As he looked over at the new arrival, a professional welcoming smile flared across his oily features. 'Well, hello, Mister Lomax. Not often we see you in here this time of day.'

With his heart suddenly pumping fit to bust, Deke Wilson only managed to remain motionless with a great effort of will. The one response he did allow himself was to let his eyes drift casually over to the large and ornate mirror behind the bar. Through it, he beheld a tall man with neatly trimmed grey hair, who didn't appear at all happy at having his name announced in such a fashion.

Ben Lomax cursed inwardly, but tried hard to avoid displaying his annoyance. After all, even in the highly unlikely event that this fellow was investigating the killings in Mammoth, he couldn't have any names. So, ambling casually over to the bar, he managed to produce something between a grimace and a smile. Yet even as he finally replied, the surveyor was favouring the stranger with sidelong scrutiny. 'Ain't that the truth, Bob? But I just had a sudden hankering for a shot of your sipping whiskey, is all.'

Bob swiftly produced another glass. 'You always did have good taste,' he replied smoothly. 'And as I was just telling this other fella, this stuff is the best there is.'

After making quite a show of tasting the amber liquid, Lomax forced an amenable expression onto his features and turned to face the weathered stranger. 'He's not wrong, you know. This even puts nectar in the shade.'

Wilson turned slowly to face the other man, and their eyes met for the first time. For long moments he just stared at him, and when he did finally respond, it wasn't anything like Lomax had expected. 'You must have mighty deep pockets, to be able to drink Buffalo Trace regularly. In a town like this, that must make you out to be a railroad man. Someone with heft who gets to give orders . . . to all sorts of people.'

Lomax tried hard to conceal his surprise, but a rapid blinking of the eyes momentarily gave him away. Such a reply had constituted far more than just a casual chinwag. His original intention had been to merely shadow this newcomer, but thanks to that fool Bob, he'd already gone way beyond all that. So, such being the case, he might as well push back a little.

'Well, if that's what fine liquor says about me, what does all that blood on your sleeves say about you?'

It wasn't lost on either man that the relaxed chatter in the saloon abruptly died away, and if they'd been watching they'd have seen uneasy puzzlement registering on the bartender's fleshy face. He was a man who could recognize trouble brewing when he saw it. As Wilson turned to face Lomax slowly, it occurred to the scout that it was getting so as he couldn't even have a quiet drink in peace.

'Well, I'll tell you, Mister Lomax. It says that Yellowstone Park is getting to be a real dangerous place.' With that, he innocently proffered his left arm for inspection, as though there was something worth viewing, and the railroad man just couldn't help himself. As he peered curiously down at the hairy sleeve, Wilson bunched his right fist and planted a tremendous blow squarely on his victim's nose. The resulting crunch could be heard all around the room.

Lomax was a big man, and so managed to stay on his feet . . . just. But any possibility he had of defending himself was already gone, especially as Wilson was taking no chances. Stepping to one side, the scout neatly kicked the other's feet from under him, taking him down like a falling tree. The surveyor hit the floorboards with a tremendous thump that completely knocked the wind from his lungs. And yet, as he lay on his back like a stranded fish, his ordeal still wasn't over. Bending down, Wilson flipped him over smartly and placed a heavy boot in the small of his back. As Frank White's regulars looked on in amazement, first the newcomer drew his Colt Revolver, and then a set of wrist irons.

'You, barkeep,' he snarled, 'get round that counter and fasten these on him. Now! Any of you sons of bitches wants to step in, think again, 'cause I'll shoot you where you stand!'

The casual drinkers obviously all had loved ones and dependants because, as Bob complied reluctantly, no one chose to move against the menacing stranger. Down on the floor, Lomax, now with his arms restrained behind his back, was in some considerable trouble. Although desperately attempting to cough up

131

blood from his broken nose, he was simultaneously struggling to draw air into his parched lungs.

'Get him on his feet, Bob,' Wilson barked.

'Why me?' that individual whined foolishly.

'Because you gave the cockchafer away, so it's the least you can do for him,' Wilson retorted. 'And after all, you wouldn't want him dying on your premises, now, would you?'

Together they dragged Lomax to his feet, and the bartender had the sense to hold him in place while he finally caught his breath. Wilson retrieved his rifles, and then gazed cynically at his unwilling assistant. 'I don't suppose you got any reliable law in this town?'

Bob stared at him in astonishment. 'After what you've just done, why would you even ask? Come to think of it, what did just happen here, and who the hell are you?'

It suddenly occurred to the scout that there was little point in lying. 'I work for the US Army out of Mammoth. This cuss is responsible for a number of murders, and he's now my prisoner.'

The bartender snorted derisively. 'I ain't never heard such foolishness. Mister Lomax is an important man in these parts. You can't just sashay in here and beat seven shades of shit out of him!'

Wilson sighed impatiently. 'I'm asking you again. Who carries the law in this burg?'

'Marshal Devereaux, but he ain't gonna back you against Mister Lomax. Livingston only exists because of the railroad.'

'Devereaux, huh?' Wilson pondered. 'Sounds kind of fancy.'

'Well, he ain't,' Bob scoffed. 'And don't ask me to try spelling his name. It's a bitch!'

With his prisoner now breathing properly, Wilson knew he had to make a move. Just what, though, was another matter entirely. His hand had been forced, and he needed time to regroup. 'I want two things from you, and then I'm out of your life. Where does this bull turd sleep nights?'

Bob glanced at Lomax and then back to the stranger. He had no inclination to cooperate, but this fella had a real dangerous air about him, as though killing was in his blood. 'Back over the tracks, to the south of town. He's got a log cabin on its own that's all his.'

Wilson nodded grimly. That made sense. Lomax had obviously spotted him on the way in. 'That's where we'll be then. Now, you go tell the marshal what occurred here. Tell him I want to talk but that he's to keep his gun holstered. Tell him.' With that, he seized the manacles and shoved Lomax towards the door roughly.

The surveyor spat a great gobbet of blood onto the wooden floor, and in a heavily nasal tone snarled, 'Whoever you are, mister, you're a dead man!'

Wilson favoured him with a genuine chuckle. 'If I'd got a dollar for every time some cockchafer said that to me, I'd own this town now, not you!'

* * *

Although feeling desperately empty inside, Captain Moses Harris nonetheless glanced over at his companion and nodded reassuringly. A few moments earlier, they had discovered Charlie Allard's frozen corpse some distance from the now stone cold fire, and both had been consumed immediately by raw anger and shock. The sight of four more bloodied, but thankfully unknown, cadavers had nevertheless compounded their emotion.

'If this don't beat all, sir,' Private Price muttered numbly. He was a fresh-faced, sandy-haired young man, who Harris had already marked out for future promotion. 'First all those dead buffalo and now this.'

Before reaching the encampment, the two men had skied past a sickening array of headless creatures whose copious bloodstains were still visible despite the recent light snowfall. The trophy heads, awaiting future recovery, hung

135

from trees a short distance away, a sickening reminder of just why Company M had been posted to Yellowstone in the first place.

'Looks like these fellas paid the ultimate penalty for their crimes,' the captain replied softly. Then he suddenly spotted a collection of carefully arranged brass cartridge cases, only thinly covered by snow. Poling forward eagerly, he gazed down at the single word message, and grunted with relief. 'Well, at least Deke survived all this intact; thank God. And now we know exactly where we're headed.' Glancing up at the sky, he added, 'We've got a little daylight left, so we might as well make the best of it.'

Side by side, the two soldiers skied off across the freezing landscape, heading north. Unbeknown to them, they were now in a race to reach Livingston before a certain hired killer by the name of Tatum. And who won that race could have great bearing on whether Deke Wilson lived or died!

Marshal Bill Devereaux stared at the bartender in disbelief. The greasy cuss had just informed him that the Northern Pacific's chief surveyor was being held prisoner in his own log cabin by some cold-eyed drifter who nobody had ever seen before. It took a conscious effort to hold back a belly laugh, because the lawman had never really taken to Ben Lomax. He considered him to be arrogant and aloof, but there could be no ignoring the fact that he worked for the railroad, and without that organisation Livingston wouldn't even exist. Devereaux considered himself to be relatively honest, but he had served his time in the tough cattle towns and valued the comfy lifestyle that he now enjoyed. In essence, he knew which side his bread was buttered!

'He said he worked for the army, but what do I know?' Bob added helpfully.

'Yeah, what *do* you know?' Devereaux muttered half to himself, then, much louder, 'He say anything else?'

137

'Yeah. You was to keep your gun holstered when you go for a parley.'

'Huh. He said that, did he?' the marshal sniffed. Then he made directly for the gun rack fastened to a sidewall of his office. Unlocking the securing chain that threaded through the trigger guards, he removed and loaded a double-barrelled sawn-off shotgun. 'I've yet to see the holster that'll hold this crowd-pleaser, and I don't jump to the tune of any passing gun thug.' So saying, he brushed past the startled bartender and on out of the building.

As Bob watched the hard-nosed lawman stride across the street, a calculating smile spread across his features. This was going to be very interesting!

★　★　★

'Just hold it right there, Marshal!' Deke Wilson commanded, aiming his Sharps directly at the approaching figure. He had no intention of allowing a sawn-off to get up close.

138

The lawman didn't slacken his pace, and so Wilson lowered the muzzle slightly and fired. The immensely powerful gun crashed out, and a great clump of dirt and slush kicked up near Devereaux's feet. That man came to a grinding halt and, greatly aggrieved, glared over at the cabin. 'What the hell you got there? Some kind of cannon?'

His ears ringing from the discharge, Wilson rapidly dropped the breechblock and replaced the long cartridge. 'The next one takes your head off. And believe me, you won't be the first law dog I've kilt!'

Devereaux pondered for a moment and then sighed. It wasn't good policy for a lawman to display any weakness. And yet, although very conscious that the gunshot was attracting a number of curious onlookers, he had no desire to call the bluff of such an obviously dangerous man. Breaking the shotgun reluctantly, he draped it over his left shoulder. 'Bob said you want to talk. So talk.'

Wilson, standing in the partially

open doorway, quickly glanced back at the heavy wooden bed in the corner of the room. Lomax, his eyes now badly bruised, was manacled to the solid frame. Helpless and hurting, all he could do was glare at his captor.

'My name is Deke Wilson,' the scout began. 'This Lomax fella is my prisoner. He ordered the murder of a poacher in the guardhouse at Mammoth, and as a result a soldier died there as well. Since then, there have been more killings. I work for the US Army, and I aim to take him back to the post. What happens after that is for someone else to decide.'

As he absorbed all this, Devereaux's eyes widened dramatically. He'd heard some tall stories in his time, but this beat all. 'And I guess you can prove all this,' he replied with great scepticism.

'Right now, none of it,' Wilson admitted forthrightly. 'But Captain Moses Harris of the 1st Cavalry sure can. He has his own prisoner in Mammoth who's talked a bucketful.' Even as he said it, he prayed that that was actually the case.

Behind him, and unobserved by the scout, Ben Lomax went rigid with shock. His ill-advised decision to have Potts killed could quite easily result in him swinging from a rope. No amount of money was worth that. And yet, right now, the only thing standing between him and freedom was this god-damned Wilson. 'This fella's got shit for brains, Marshal,' he bellowed out suddenly. Ignoring his own blood spattering over his clothes, he gave it his best shot. 'Why would I, of all people, want to kill some no-account poacher? It doesn't make any sense. You can't let him do this. It just ain't right. He's already broken my dose, for Christ's sake!'

Had Deke Wilson been nearer, he'd have used the butt of his rifle to break something else. As it was, he had to keep watch on the lawman and await his response. It wasn't long in coming.

'This is what's gonna happen, Wilson. You release Mister Lomax into my custody and go get your evidence. Then I'll decide who has the right of it. He'll be quite safe in my jail 'til you return. You have my oath on that.'

The scout had been half expecting a suggestion like that. 'No deal, Marshal!'

'Then you ain't moving from there,' came the rapid retort.

'An' likewise, you ain't coming in here.' Their exchange was becoming increasingly childish. It was time to end it. 'Seems like we'll just have to wait on events,' Wilson announced, and then slammed and barred the door. Turning, he found Lomax staring up at him, a pensive expression on his mangled features.

'How much to let me walk? Every man's got a price, and yours can't be that high.'

Wilson didn't miss the quite probably unintended insult in that, and his blood began to boil. 'My advice to you, cock-chafer, is to hold your goddamn tongue. I intend to see what the new day brings, which means we've got a long night ahead of us. And you don't want me beating on that face of yours again!'

8

The Eighth Day

Tatum was in a foul mood as he finally trudged into Livingston early that morning. His arm was aching so much that he suspected the flesh wound could be infected. So preoccupied was he that he passed within yards of Ben Lomax's cabin without even realizing the fact. The subject uppermost on his mind was hard liquor, and plenty of it, poured both down his throat and on his injury. All of which meant that his immediate destination had to be Frank White's saloon, because it was common knowledge that that establishment served the best hard liquor in town.

Reaching those premises, he found that the heavy door remained stubbornly closed against any reasonable pressure. Seizing his knife angrily, Tatum repeatedly slammed its hilt against the obstruction. Long minutes passed, until he decided that he'd just have to kick the damn thing in. Then, abruptly, Bob's sullen features appeared behind the glass in the upper section of the door. Very reluctantly, that individual eased the bolts back.

'Hell, you're making enough noise to wake snakes, mister,' he complained peevishly. It was far too early in the day for him, and so he hadn't yet given the newcomer a good once over. 'Thing is, we're not open yet.'

'You are now!' the other man snarled, shouldering his way into the saloon roughly. 'Whiskey, and plenty of it. And not the cheap swill, either. I got money, see, so be quick about it!' In support of his demands, he brandished his knife under Bob's nose. The bartender, suddenly realizing that he had a hardcase on the premises, scurried behind the counter without another word.

As a bottle of Buffalo Trace appeared before him, Tatum eased his heavy coat off, and then gingerly cut the bloodied underclothes away from his torn flesh. The wound was red and angry, but mercifully didn't stink of greenrod. Steeling himself against the inevitable shock, he upended the bottle over it.

'Holy shit!' he howled, as he performed an agonised jig in front of the bar. That was followed immediately by a long, satisfying swig of the strong liquor. Bob glanced unhappily at the unholy mix of whiskey and blood on his counter, but wisely remained silent.

'Is Ben Lomax in town?' the gun thug demanded abruptly.

Bob twitched with surprise. 'Hah. He can't rightly leave.'

Tatum was in no mood for riddles. 'Say what?'

The bartender, now with valuable information to impart, felt rather more secure. Warming to his subject gradually, he related the unusual happenings of the previous afternoon in their entirety.

★ ★ ★

A short while later, Marshal Devereaux glanced up impatiently from the bowl of fresh bread and piping hot beans that constituted his breakfast. He didn't like being disturbed by any callers so early in the day, and sadly this evil-looking cuss sure didn't seem to be paying a social visit. The stranger appeared to be on the prod, and what he said immediately confirmed that supposition.

'This tarnal cockchafer, Wilson. Why's he still alive?'

Devereaux blinked, before swallowing a half-chewed mouthful uncomfortably. 'He says he works for the army. He's got Lomax under his gun, and states that man has blood on his hands. He says he's got proof.'

'That's pure hogwash!' barked Tatum. 'The bastard jumped me and five others while we was asleep down in the park. They're all dead, every last mother's son of them. He'd have kilt me too, if'en I hadn't hightailed it.' Displaying his sleeve, he added, 'This is my blood. My bona fides.'

The lawman gazed at him askance. He could smell the whiskey on this pus weasel's breath, and he could also recognize bullshit when he heard it. 'Just what were all of you fellas doing in Yellowstone this time of year? And why would he even want to jump six of you? All sounds pretty thin to me.'

Tatum tapped the side of his nose. 'We were there on railroad business,' he replied shortly, as though that explained everything. 'And without the railroad, this shithole wouldn't exist, and you'd be out of a nice little job, *Marshal*. It would behove you to remember that!'

Devereaux bridled at the other's tone. Livingston was actually as nice a place to live as he had come across, and he'd seen plenty in his time. But one thing this unpleasant son of a bitch had said was true. The lawman *did* have a cushy number, and he dearly wanted to retain it. 'So just what are you asking of me?' he enquired reluctantly.

Tatum was all too aware that this Wilson could genuinely be waiting on the arrival of some boys in blue. If that happened, Lomax was screwed, and along with him went a good source of income. It was time to breach the peace! 'You're the only one badged up in this town,' he replied meaningfully. 'So it's time to get off of your ass and earn your corn!'

The marshal uttered a deep sigh. Somehow, he had known it would come down to this. 'He's got Lomax chained up in there, an' he's toting a couple of buffalo guns that he knows how to use.' If he had expected that disclosure to deter the other man, then he was to be sorely disappointed.

'It's mighty cold, so there'll be a fire burning in Lomax's stove,' Tatum opined. 'We just tip some coal oil down the chimney and rush the place.' That was said so matter-of-factly that it might have been something he did every day.

'That sounds risky as hell,' replied Devereaux dubiously.

'So's living!'

★ ★ ★

There had been a most distinct and one-sided division of the spoils in Lomax's cabin, and consequently he was a very unhappy man. Deke Wilson had passed a comfortable night on the only cot, whereas his prisoner had been chained to one of the legs of the cast iron stove. Likewise, breakfast had been a very biased affair of bacon, beans and coffee for one. It was only now that the red-eyed and badly bruised surveyor got a turn on the cot, and then only because he was manacled to it. A consequence of his sleepless night was that he'd had plenty of time to think, and there was one big question preying on Lomax's unquiet mind.

'So who've you got locked away in Mammoth dat's giving testimony against me?' he demanded, the broken nose badly affecting his speech.

Wilson was loading the stove with fresh firewood. As anger flared up within him, he turned away, and in the process neglected to close it properly. As he replied, his expression was icy. 'Is that so he might end up like Potts and that fine young soldier you had butchered?'

Lomax sighed uncomfortably. 'Dat was a mistake.'

'Damn right it was, railroad man. The biggest one you'll ever make. And think on this. If that lawman should decide that he's somehow beholden to the Northern Pacific and tries something foolish, you won't even get to see the inside of a courtroom!'

At that very moment, as though by divine timing, Marshal Devereaux's voice boomed out beyond the cabin door. 'There's been a turn of events, Wilson. You and me need to parley.'

'Talk of the devil and he often appears,' that man muttered.

Then, ever methodical, the scout pulled on his heavy coat, placed the Remington by the side of the threshold, and finally cocked his Sharps. Only then did he open the door and call out. 'Same deal as before, Marshal. Don't go pointing any firearms in my direction.'

If he hadn't been occupied, he might just have heard a ladder being placed against the rear of the cabin. As it was, the only person who did was Lomax, and he didn't quite know what to make of the footsteps he then heard on the roof. Chained to the cot, he felt distinctly vulnerable.

'We need to find a way out of this mess,' Devereaux remarked smoothly, displaying more composure than he actually felt. 'You can't stay holed up in there forever.'

Up on the roof, Tatum had his Winchester across his back and a jug of kerosene in his hands. He hadn't been able to locate any coal oil, but what the hell; this other stuff would surely answer. Smoke drifted out of the iron chimney that connected directly to the stove. It was a long while since he'd had cause to do this sort of thing, and the prospect tickled him. In the middle of winter, there was nothing better than a good fire to keep a man warm ... except maybe a woman. Any kind of woman, from anywhere! Sighing wistfully, he kept the jug at arm's length and upended it over the chimney mouth.

Wilson, standing to one side of the open door, felt a vague uneasiness come over him. This pesky lawman apparently had nothing new to offer, so why stand around in the cold for no good reason? Behind him, and without any warning, the stove suddenly seemed to explode with a tremendous *whumph*. As a sheet of flame blew out of the unsecured iron door, the scout acted purely on instinct. Seizing his spare rifle, he threw himself onto the ground in front of the cabin. His natural preference was to confront whatever awaited him outside, than to be trapped inside a burning building.

As he hit the ground, Wilson saw Devereaux close the shotgun's breech and swing the gaping muzzles towards him. So much for the lawman's impartiality! Up on the roof, Tatum had tossed the empty keg behind him into the snow. He now swung the Winchester from over his shoulder and drew a bead on the *hombre* who had shot him back in the park. 'You're a dead man,' he muttered venomously.

Oblivious of the deadly threat at his rear, and faced with both loads from a twelve gauge, the army scout reacted like a well-oiled machine. Cocking the Sharps, he didn't take deliberate aim, but instead merely pointed it at Devereaux's torso and squeezed both triggers . . . hard. With awesome force, the .50 calibre bullet slammed into the marshal's right shoulder at the very instant his forefinger closed over the sawn-off's triggers. Staggering back under the tremendous impact, he unwittingly jerked the big gun up just as both barrels discharged. Accompanied by a massive roar, the lethal spread of shot mostly whistled off into fresh air. Mostly!

Even as Wilson rolled to his right, there came an unexpected scream of pain from above and behind. That was followed by another gunshot, and a bullet smacked into the ground a few feet away. Realizing that his current position was untenable, the scout scrambled to his feet, and ran full pelt for the nearest cabin. He didn't attempt to enter it. All he needed was its solid wall for cover. Reaching it, he then became the third point on a triangle formed by the three antagonists. It was only then that he perceived the frantic cries for help emanating from the building he had just vacated.

Almost incandescent with rage, Tatum pawed at the blood streaming from a deep cut on the side of his head. Being at the extreme edge of the shot pattern, he had been exceptionally lucky, but of course didn't see it that way. 'Who's side are you on?' he bellowed indignantly at the suffering lawman.

With the now muddy Remington still over his shoulder, Wilson reloaded his Sharps swiftly and glanced over at Lomax's cabin. Flames from the stove had obviously taken hold inside because smoke was now billowing out of the open door. Above, on the reverse side of the pitched roof, a lone figure holding a long gun was just visible. His face was streaked with fresh blood, presumably as a result of the wild shotgun blast.

'You must be Tatum,' Wilson hollered over. 'You're wanted by the US Army for murder.'

'Reckon I'm right popular,' that man retorted, pain clearly discernable in his voice.

From Wilson's right flank, and hidden by his new shelter, Devereaux yelled out with great indignation. 'What the hell did you just use on me, you son of a bitch? I ain't some kind of buffalo!'

Wilson scampered to the other end of the cabin wall and peered around. The wounded and very dejected lawman had collapsed onto his ass in the mud. His right shoulder was soaked with blood and he showed no signs of trying to continue the fight. To encourage that attitude, Wilson yelled back, 'There's one hundred and ten grains of powder behind each bullet, you cockchafer. Point another gun in my direction an' I'll send a second at you!'

'And that goes for me too, you dozy bastard,' Tatum added angrily. 'You nearly kilt me with that damn scattergun!'

Without waiting for any reply, the army scout retraced his steps and only narrowly avoided having his head blown off. The gun thug on the roof, having mopped the blood from his face, opened up with his Winchester to great effect. As bullet after bullet slammed into timber, a nasty splinter scored Wilson's left cheek. Cursing volubly, he waited for a lull in the shooting and then took rapid aim with his Sharps. As his shoulder absorbed the brutal recoil, the heavy bullet tore a large chunk of wood out of the roof next to Tatum. With an oath, that man instinctively ducked back out of sight.

Then, abruptly, everything changed, as Ben Lomax's insistent cries for help became screams of pain. The fire had taken hold on the cabin, and was spreading throughout its interior. Smoke rose up through chinks in the roof, and tongues of flame licked the threshold.

'For pity's sake, someone help me!' the captive surveyor wailed as he tugged helplessly against the manacle.

'Your boss will burn to death in there,' Wilson yelled over. 'If you throw down your guns, I'll hold fire while you set him free. You have my word on that. I'll even toss you the key to the irons.'

'Too thin, mister. Too thin,' Tatum retorted. 'He ain't my problem, and I sure ain't risking my skin for him. I reckon I'll just have to find a new employer, is all.'

Wilson sighed. He personally wasn't about to attempt a rescue, but he really had wanted Lomax alive. Now, if that wasn't to be, he would at least avenge Private Lane Turner. His killer was up on a roof that was about to be consumed by flames. All the scout had to do was wait.

Inside the burning structure, a tremendous commotion occurred, as Lomax made a final, frantic attempt to break free. There was no planning behind it, because any opportunity for rational thought had passed. All he could do was thrash about, and yet he nearly made it. Even as flesh blistered on his face and hands, the desperate individual managed to heave the cot on its side and drag it to the door. But then it got tangled around the heavy iron stove. Blinded with pain, all he could do was tug ineffectually at the manacle on his wrist that was now slick with blood, but still he was held fast. If he could have cut his own hand off he would have done so. But even such terrible action wouldn't have saved him, because at that moment his clothes caught fire, and suddenly it was all over for Ben Lomax.

'Why don't one of you try to save him?' Devereaux roared. Badly hampered by his shoulder wound, and yet genuinely sickened by the surveyor's gruesome fate, he was attempting to stand up ineffectually.

No one answered him, because the only two that could have intervened were too busy trying to kill each other. Tatum loosed off another shot from his vantage point, but he was uncomfortably aware that he couldn't remain on the roof much longer. Flames were curling around the outside of the cabin. Then all sounds of life from below abruptly ceased. Apparently he was, and not for the first time in his violent career, now out of a job.

* * *

A crowd of onlookers had gathered at a supposedly safe distance to observe the unusual spectacle being played out before them. Such brutal, bloody violence was, for the majority of them, a thankfully rare occurrence in Livingston. Mostly it was just the odd drunken brawl. And yet, there were a good few for whom the spectacular confrontation was a welcome respite from a too often joyless winter.

If all the good citizens hadn't been so preoccupied, they just might have noticed two more new arrivals skiing vigorously from the direction of Yellowstone Park. As it was, their rapt attention remained on the burning building and the lone gunman on top of it.

* * *

With flames now curling around the edges of the roof, it was definitely time to get back down the ladder, before that too caught fire. Working the lever action with practised speed, Tatum sent a stream of hot lead towards his opponent. At relatively close range, the repeater gave him a sure advantage over the single shot buffalo guns.

'God damn that Winchester,' Wilson muttered, as he backed away from the blizzard of splinters.

Up on the roof, Tatum decided that the moment was right. Even with strong footwear, his feet could feel the heat coming up through the timber. Clutching his rifle, the now unemployed hired gun quickly retreated to the waiting ladder. Swinging onto it, he descended rapidly to safety, and then paused at the bottom to reload. He had a choice to make:

whether to hightail it, or renew the now unprofitable fight against his all too obviously capable adversary. Cartridges cost money, and he was no longer on wages. Deep in thought, he didn't actually hear the movement behind him. It was some form of sixth sense that alerted him, but whatever it was it was too damn late.

Tatum twisted around like a cat . . . just in time to receive the butt of a Springfield Carbine on his already bloodied forehead. The stunning blow was sufficient to send him to his knees. Through watering eyes, the gun thug dimly perceived two shapes looming before him.

'You're under arrest!' one of the figures remarked brusquely. Tatum instinctively muttered some foul obscenity, and was rewarded by another shattering blow to his temple. As his eyes closed, he fell face first into the melting snow.

* * *

Deke Wilson waited until he could see flames actually devouring the roof of

161

Lomax's cabin before he peered cautiously around the corner of his protective wall. Any threat now was likely to come from ground level, so he dropped down into the snow and readied his Sharps.

Quite without warning, a familiar voice suddenly called out, 'You don't have to prostrate yourself before me, Deke Wilson.'

Then there was movement from well behind the blazing cabin, and the army scout got the surprise of his life. Coming into view before him, large as life, came the imposing figure of Captain Moses Harris. As their eyes met, both men produced broad smiles, but it was Harris who provided the appropriate greeting. 'Looks like you've been having yourself quite a time!'

9

The Ninth Day

Marshal Bill Devereaux still found his change in circumstances hard to believe. A mere two days earlier, he had been the sole lawman of a mostly quiet railroad town without any apparent threat to his authority. Now he had a goddamn hole in his shoulder the size of a railroad tunnel, which had yet to decide whether to infect or not. The pain from it was just awful. On top of that, he no longer had control over his own jailhouse and didn't even possess the key to the cell that held the only prisoner. And as if all that wasn't enough, the chief surveyor of the Northern Pacific had been burnt to a crisp . . . not that anyone in Livingston was likely to miss him!

To add insult to undoubted injury, there was even a permanent sentry on the premises in the form of Private Price. Presumably, this precaution was to ensure that the marshal didn't try anything stupid. As if he could, what with his arm in a sling an' all.

The sawbones had bound his shoulder up so tightly that it felt like he wouldn't ever be able to move it again.

Devereaux glanced up sourly as the jailhouse door opened. And here was this god-damned blue belly officer sashaying around as though he owned the place. The presence of the soldier's companion was even more galling. The man had shot him, for Christ's sake! He glowered up at Wilson, but that man was unrepentant.

'Don't look sideways at me, law dog. You called it!'

The marshal wasn't the only disaffected occupant of the jailhouse. Tatum, bloodstained and heavily bruised about the face, had plenty to say. 'You sons of bitches ain't got anything to hold me on. The most you're allowed do is throw me out of Yellowstone for poaching . . . an' we're *already* out!'

Captain Harris only maintained his

164

deadpan expression with difficulty. The gun thug was quite correct, and that knowledge rankled. It rankled a great deal. And the poacher, Garfield, who was hopefully still locked up in Mammoth, could only really provide hearsay rather than hard evidence. However, it was then that Deke Wilson proved he was far more than just a good scout and manhunter.

'I reckon killing Lomax is grounds to keep you locked up.'

Tatum's eyes widened dramatically. 'It was the fire kilt him, not me!'

Wilson favoured him with a mirthless smile. 'There's plenty of witnesses saw you tip kerosene down the chimney . . . including the town marshal. Ain't that right, *Marshal*?'

That individual's face suddenly became a battleground of conflicting emotions. Fear, greed and raw cunning all came into play. 'I just might have seen something of the sort,' he finally replied, taking care to avoid Tatum's hate filled gaze.

'All of which will be enough to hang you, mister,' Wilson abruptly snarled at the startled prisoner.

'Unless, of course, you're prepared to tell all that you know, under oath, about what Lomax was really up to out here,' Harris quickly added. Then, having given Tatum something to think about, he gestured for the scout to follow him outside. Only then, when there was no possibility of them being overheard, did he continue. 'It's my considered belief that the Secretary of the Interior is involved in all this.'

The revelation shocked Wilson, who had no knowledge whatsoever of the machinations of government. As a consequence he was unusually slow on the uptake. 'What the hell for?' he managed.

The officer was in no doubt. 'Greed, of course. Politicians are always trying to get their noses in the trough. Back in the '70s, President Grant's administration was riddled with corruption. Think about it. There'd be a fortune to make out of Cooke City, *if* it could be connected to the railroad. All that silver ore, waiting to be turned into hard cash. The only problem is, there just happens to be a national park slap bang in the way. Very inconvenient!'

Wilson nodded ruefully. 'I must have led a sheltered life, out on the frontier. All I know how to do is track and kill things.'

Harris favoured him with a genuinely warm smile. 'Don't sell yourself short, Deke. You're a good man.'

'Thank you kindly, Captain,' the other man replied softly. He appeared sincerely pleased by the unexpected praise. 'So what are your intentions? Because you do always seem to have some kind of plan.'

'Hah, they say God laughs at those who make plans. But anyway, I intend to send a couple of telegraphs and then see what occurs.'

'You mean you're going to stir some shit.' There was a stubborn set to Harris's jaw that the scout had seen before. 'Something like that.'

'Are you really sure you want to do that?'

'Protecting the park, and everything that's in it, is what we're out here for,' Harris countered. 'And besides, Private Turner deserves justice.'

Wilson nodded his agreement. 'Yeah, well, I suppose it has been a bit quiet recently, being as how there's no Indians to fight anymore!'

TO SECRETARY OF THE INTERIOR LAMAR *STOP* HAVE APPREHENDED PRIVATE TURNER'S KILLER IN LIVINGSTON *STOP* INTEND TO DISCOVER HIS MOTIVATION *STOP* SURVEYOR BEN LOMAX DEAD *STOP* WILL KEEP YOU INFORMED *STOP* CAPTAIN HARRIS — MILITARY SUPERINTENDENT *STOP* TO COMMANDING GENERAL SHERIDAN *STOP* BELIEVE I HAVE UNCOVERED PLOT TO DISCREDIT THE NEED FOR

AND REMOVE FROM EXIST-
ENCE THE NORTH-EASTERN
SECTION OF YELLOWSTONE
NATIONAL PARK *STOP*
BELIEVE INTENTION IS TO
PUSH RAILROAD THROUGH
TO SILVER WORKINGS NEAR
COOKE CITY *STOP* THIS HAS
SO FAR CAUSED A NUM-
BER OF FATALITIES *STOP* IN
POSSESSION OF PRISONER
IN LIVINGSTON WHO CAN
CONFIRM THIS *STOP* HAVE
ONLY TWO MEN IN SUPPORT
STOP ASSISTANCE WOULD BE
APPRECIATED *STOP* CAPTAIN
MOSES HARRIS — MILITARY
SUPERINTENDENT *STOP*

The two prosperous-looking, frock-coated men stood in a quiet corner of the back yard of Mades' Restaurant, apparently pondering over which poor creature to choose from the frog pond. Sadly, in reality, such culinary delights couldn't have been further from their minds.

'This is all getting completely out of hand,' Secretary Lamar opined in a heated whisper. 'Lomax has been killed, for God's sake!'

Jay Cooke shrugged. 'Can't make a cake without breaking eggs. Did your telegram say how?'

'No.'

'Well, then, it could have been an accident.

For all we know, he could have been mauled by a grizzly.'

Lamar gritted his teeth. His companion's apparent insouciance was seriously getting under his craw. 'So tell me this. Why would Phil Sheridan be asking me questions about Yellowstone and the Northern Pacific Railroad shortly after I received Harris's telegram? I've got a bad feeling this is all going to blow up in our faces!'

For the first time, a trace of anxiety showed on Cooke's normally smug features. The commanding general, a famous Civil War veteran, was notoriously feisty and incorruptible, and known for his voluble support of the nation's first national park. If he got involved, there could indeed be serious repercussions. If there was anything to investigate, of course. 'Don't you have anyone in the area who could possibly *remove* this tiresome witness?'

Lucius Lamar momentarily assumed a slightly superior air. 'After Harris's first telegram, I took the precaution of sending some men to Columbus. It's a railroad town, just to the east of Livingston.'

'I have heard of it,' Cooke retorted testily. It was becoming obvious that this affair was actually beginning to work on his nerves a little. 'And just who are these *men*?'

'I have used them before. They formerly worked for the Justice Department. They're problem solvers. You'll be paying their fee.' Lamar added pointedly, before pausing and staring hard at the financier. 'And on the subject of money, I want your word that if this all goes wrong, and I have to resign, you will support me financially. I'm not a wealthy man, as you know. That's why I got involved in this scheme in the first place.'

Jay Cooke's eyes glazed over slightly, as though he was suddenly getting bored, but nevertheless he managed to summon a reassuring smile. 'Don't you trouble yourself, Lucius. I would never abandon a friend in need.'

It was to be some time later that Secretary Lamar would recall that he had never yet heard of anyone who referred to the businessman as 'friend'.

TO CAPTAIN HARRIS — LIVINGSTON *STOP* I HAVE ORDERED CIVILIAN AUTHORITIES TO REMOVE YOUR PRISONER *STOP* THEY SHOULD BE WITH YOU SOMETIME TOMORROW *STOP* ONCE THIS TRANSFER HAS TAKEN PLACE YOU WILL RETURN TO MAMMOTH AT ONCE *STOP* YOUR

ASSISTANCE IN THIS MATTER
WILL NOT GO UNNOTICED
STOP LUCIUS LAMAR — SEC-
RETARY TO THE INTERIOR
STOP

'*Lucius* Lamar,' Harris scoffed. 'It's the first time that son of a bitch has used his given name with me.'

It was late in the afternoon, and the officer and his scout were nursing their drinks in a quiet corner of Frank White's saloon. The bartender, uncomfortably aware of his earlier assistance to Tatum, was keeping well clear. Besides, uniforms of any kind made him nervous at the best of times.

Wilson had just read the telegram, and had his own take on the contents. 'Seems kind of convenient that he has men only a day's travel away. Him being in Washington an' all.'

'Doesn't it just?' Harris agreed, before then handing over the second telegram that he had received.

TO CAPTAIN HARRIS—
LIVINGSTON *STOP* ALL
MATTERS CONCERNING YEL-
LOWSTONE NATIONAL PARK
ARE CLOSE TO MY HEART *STOP*
THIS PARTICULAR AFFAIR
DEFINITELY WARRANTS FUR-
THER INVESTIGATION *STOP*
I HAVE ORDERED MY STAFF
OFFICER MAJOR TRUMBALL
SMITH AND A DETAIL OF
MEN TO JOIN YOU IN LIV-
INGSTON *STOP* UNDER NO
CIRCUMSTANCES WILL YOU
RELEASE YOUR PRISONER
TO ANY OTHER AUTHORITY
STOP GOOD WORK CAPTAIN
STOP LIEUTENANT GENERAL
SHERIDAN — WASHINGTON
STOP

Wilson's eyebrows rose expressively.
'Hot dang! Don't that beat all?'

'Does kind of make you think, doesn't
it?' Harris responded with a wry smile.

'D'you reckon they're coming to kill

him?' the scout pondered. 'Or just drag him off in chains?'

The officer didn't hesitate. 'It makes no difference. We can't allow Lamar's men to do either.'

'So what are you ... *we* gonna do, Captain?'

Harris's voice dropped almost to a whisper, although in truth there was no one near enough to overhear. His next words proved that he had given their predicament a great deal of thought. 'Well, first off, we know that both groups will arrive by train, because they must have received their instructions by telegram, and all the telegraph lines run next to railroad tracks. I've no idea where this Major Smith is coming from, but Lamar's men are most likely coming from somewhere to the east of here. Somewhere close, like Billings or maybe even Columbus. If their intention is to kill Tatum, we can't leave him in the jailhouse. His cell is merely to keep him incarcerated, and certainly isn't proof against assassins' bullets. And that goddamn marshal is neither use nor ornament. So we need to check with the depot to find out when the next trains are due, and then find somewhere more defensible.'

'What about this place?' Wilson asked, as he peered around the saloon. 'We could stash the son of a bitch on the floor behind the bar. It looks solid enough.'

'Question is, would it stop a bullet?' Harris mused.

A broad smile suddenly appeared on Wilson's face. In one fluid movement, he drew, cocked, aimed and fired his revolver. In such an enclosed space, the report was ear-splittingly loud. The bullet slammed into the bar just below the counter. Those other drinkers in the room gazed around in surprise, but none of them seemed inclined to flee.

'What in tarnation are you about?' the bartender demanded angrily.

'You just hush now, Bob,' the scout retorted. 'Or I might just aim the next one over your way. I know it was you told that gun thug where to find me.'

The captain stood up and moved purposefully towards the counter. He soon spotted the disfigured piece of lead, wedged tightly in the thick wood. Nodding with satisfaction, he turned to the bartender. 'You got a back door to this place?'

Bob peered at him suspiciously. 'Of course.'

'Show me.'

A few moments later, the officer sat back down next to Wilson, ignoring the curious glances of the other patrons. He chuckled. 'That greasy looking swamper is in for a shock when we commandeer this shithole!'

'You've taken to the idea, then.'

'Oh yeah, it's definitely got its charms. When you've finished sipping that whiskey, why don't you go see if the hardware store sells dynamite while I check over at the rail depot.'

'Dynamite!' Wilson exclaimed, keeping his voice low only with difficulty. 'You're sure fixing on playing rough, ain't you, Captain?'

Harris favoured him with a half-smile.

'It's been a long time since the war, and folks sometimes forget that soldiers are trained to kill. If my hunch is correct, we might just need to remind them tomorrow.'

* * *

The depot clerk gazed up at the officer with mild curiosity. It wasn't often the military came to Livingston. He'd heard all about the gunfight, of course, and Ben Lomax's particularly gruesome demise. Not that such tidings had perturbed him in the slightest. He'd never taken to the surveyor. The arrogant cuss had had a habit of treating lesser mortals with noticeable condescension.

'What trains have you got coming through here tomorrow?' Harris queried.

Although the railroad had only finally been completed about four years earlier, it seemed to have been in existence for far longer, and the Northern Pacific employee knew the timetable off by heart. 'The westbound comes in from Columbus at eleven thirty in the morning . . . *every* morning. The eastbound from Bozeman arrives at three-thirty in the afternoon . . . *every* afternoon. That's *Mountain Time*, of course,' he added officiously, keen to display his technical knowledge to a mere soldier. In his part of the world, the concept of time zones was still new enough for them to be something of a novelty.

'Uh-huh. And are they usually on time?'

The clerk appeared genuinely affronted. 'You could set your watch by them . . . if you happened to have one, that is.'

Harris's expression unexpectedly hardened. 'Would you care to bet your life on their punctuality?'

'*Sir*?'

The officer laughed suddenly. 'Just funning, mister. Just funning.' And with that, he produced a fob watch from an inside pocket abruptly and winked. 'But I could well be betting *my* life on them!'

10

The Tenth Day — Morning

The snow-covered landscape seemed to stretch into infinity, but the harsh surroundings were of little concern to the two men sitting snugly in their westbound railroad carriage. The fact that they would have had to make the journey on horseback or skis not so long before did not even occur to them because, not for the first time in their working lives, they had matters of life and death importance to discuss. Quite literally life and death!

'So what are we up against in this hick town?' Jim Coates enquired.

'Huh, believe it or not, it's the US Army,' Brett Tucker replied. 'But only some of it.'

The other man's black brows rose expressively. 'That's a first. An' just who have they upset? The rest of it?'

Tucker smiled. He was a tall, pockmarked individual, who had made his living in law enforcement until he realized there was far more money to be earned hiring his services out to the wealthy and the powerful. Since the dawn of the railroad era, there had been plenty of both. 'Secretary Lamar. Although I reckon Jay Cooke's actually bankrolling all this. Apparently, a cavalry captain by the name of Harris has arrested someone he shouldn't have. We need to persuade this fine officer to release him to us.'

'And if he won't?'

Tucker patted the Winchester Carbine leaning against the rattling windowsill, before glancing over at the six other men in the carriage. Armed to the teeth and chewing tobacco relentlessly, they all possessed a comforting aura of barely suppressed violence. 'We will act in our client's best interests, as usual.'

It was Coates's turn to smile, which in truth was something he rarely did. But there was just something about his companion's use of flowery language that tickled him. The man had a way of making an often grim and bloody occupation sound somehow respectable. 'What about the local law?' he queried.

Tucker shrugged his broad shoulders. 'Apparently there's only the one badged up. What happens to him depends on the position he adopts. If he's sensible, he'll take the day off. Other than him, there's a US Marshal, name of Robert Kelley, down the line in Billings. He's a good officer, but at this time of year, likely he'll be sat round the stove with his feet up. And however it pans out, we'll only be in town for four hours, 'cause at three-thirty we hop on the east-bound and get the hell out of Livingston . . . with or without a prisoner!'

His partner nodded approvingly. 'That's why I like working with you, Brett. You cover *all* the angles.'

'Which is why I'm still alive,' Tucker retorted smugly. He saw no reason why anything awaiting them in Livingston should change that.

★ ★ ★

'Say again?' Bob queried, all the while staring incredulously at Moses Harris.

The captain sighed. Perhaps it was the word 'commandeered' that the bartender hadn't understood. 'We're taking over these premises for the day. Clear all your customers out and give yourself a holiday.'

'You can't do that,' the other man protested. 'It ain't legal!'

'I've done it, and it is,' Harris retorted impatiently, anxious to be rid of him. 'This building is now under military jurisdiction.'

'The marshal will hear of this,' Bob retorted. 'Then we'll see.'

'I think you'll find that the marshal has got enough problems of his own,' Harris replied. 'Recognize this?' So saying, he hefted Devereaux's sawn-off so that the gaping muzzles were pointed directly at Bob's chest. 'Now move, before I forget I'm on the side of law and order.'

'Well, in that case, I'll have to tell Mister White,' the bartender protested, as he backed away towards his unhappy customers. 'He's in Billings on business, and he ain't gonna like this one little bit. I'll telegraph him there.'

'You just do that! But you can't do it in here, can you? So scat. And take everyone else along too.' By way of encouragement, he discharged one of the shotgun's barrels into the ceiling with a tremendous roar. As falling wood shavings mingled with a cloud of smoke, the bartender and his customers fled without another word.

According to the officer's fob watch, the time was ten-fifty, so whomever Lamar had sent would most likely be arriving in town in forty minutes. Sadly, he couldn't imagine that Sheridan's men would also be on the same train, so the three of them were likely on their own.

Only once the saloon was empty and he had reloaded his weapon did Harris return to the street and order Private Price to bring in the prisoner. 'Get him face down behind the bar. If there's something solid to chain him to then so much the better.'

Tatum glared sullenly at him. 'You got no right treating me this way, soldier boy. No right at all.'

'Is that so?' Harris retorted. 'Well, think on this. Whoever's coming here is quite probably under orders to kill you, rather than risk letting you talk. So we're actually trying to save your life.'

The assassin's eyes widened slightly as he digested that. It was obvious that such a possibility hadn't occurred to him. As Price led Tatum to his temporary accommodation, the door opened and Wilson appeared. He carried a rifle over each shoulder and his pockets bulged.

'Have you picked your spot, Deke?' Harris queried.

The scout nodded. 'Oh, I have, Captain. Two actually. One near the back of this place, and a last stand in one of the engine sheds. There'll be a rifle at each. If you all have to leave through the back, there won't be anyone catching you by surprise.'

The officer moved in close, and extended his right hand. 'Well, then, I suggest you take up residence, because if the train's on time we haven't got long. Good luck to you, Scout!'

'Thank you, sir,' Deke Wilson replied with uncommon formality. 'And whatever happens, it's been mighty fine working for you!'

★ ★ ★

A shrill steam whistle had just announced the departure of the westbound train when the two men strode into the jailhouse and took a long hard look around. The knowledge that they had six others outside watching their backs only added to their brazen confidence. Nevertheless, what they saw gave them pause. The door to the only cell lay wide open, and the interior was quite obviously empty. The only occupant of the office was a sad faced individual, sporting both a badge and a sling. A slight taint of blood was visible on the material, indicating that his injury was recent. Even more tellingly, the gun rack behind him was completely empty. It was as though the town marshal had been comprehensively emasculated.

Brett Tucker possessed the ability to interpret the whole scene with startling clarity. Abruptly turning his full attention to the startled lawman, he remarked, 'I'm Tucker, he's Coates. If you don't mind my saying, you seem like a pretty sorry looking sack of shit to be sat behind that desk!'

Devereaux's jaw dropped comically. He'd never heard of any sons of bitches called Coates and Tucker, and he certainly wasn't in the mood for any more insults. Yet sadly, he also wasn't in any position to retaliate. 'There ain't no cause for you fellas to abuse me,' he remarked plaintively. 'Hell, it's just all shit an' no sugar this week!' Then a thought came to him: a way of getting rid of these unwanted visitors. 'If you've come here looking for someone in particular, happen you'll find him in Frank White's saloon across the way.'

'Well, that's mighty helpful of you,

Marshal,' Tucker replied laconically. 'And what about the army? Are they in there too?'

Devereaux considered his response to that. He *was* still a peace officer, after all. But then he recalled that one of them had busted his shoulder up, and any scruples immediately dissipated. 'There's three of them, an' they're packing plenty of iron. Including my sawn-off,' he added resentfully.

'Obliged to you, Marshal,' Tucker responded amicably enough. 'We'll be leaving you now.' Then he nodded meaningfully at his companion.

Jim Coates drifted closer to the lawman's desk, and extended his left arm, as though considerately intending to shake hands on his uninjured side. Surprised at the unexpected courtesy, Devereaux reciprocated innocently. Even as he did so, Coates swiftly drew his side arm, and slammed the butt down onto the man's unprotected skull. The luckless marshal didn't even cry out; he just collapsed face first onto his desk.

As Coates seized his victim's revolver, he chuckled. 'He sure was right. It really *ain't* his week.'

With any threat to their rear now removed, the two men stepped out onto the sidewalk and looked over towards Frank White's saloon. Their six heavily muffled employees regarded them expectantly. All were professionals, and all were known personally by one or other of the leaders. Two of them toted sawn-off shotguns, whilst the others held similar versions of the ubiquitous Winchester. Beneath their heavy coats, each of the men carried at least one holster gun, along with a smaller calibre hideaway weapon and some kind of knife. None of them harboured any fears that the outcome of this task would be different to the countless others they had undertaken.

The flesh on Tucker's face seemed to tighten into a hard mask as he nodded at the others. It was time to get the job done. Without having to be told, the self-styled deputies spread out on either side of him and Coates, and they all moved steadily through the slush towards the saloon. For a supposedly thriving railroad town, the thoroughfare was eerily quiet. It was as though Livingston's citizens knew that trouble was coming. The newcomers hadn't missed the pile of ashes, south of the tracks, where a building had recently burned down, but they didn't think anything of it. Fires were not unusual out west, where settlements were mostly constructed of wood.

As the intimidating line of gunmen reached Frank White's, Tucker glanced at the two men on his extreme left. 'See if there's a back door, but don't go in. Savvy?'

As they nodded assent and moved off, he continued. 'The rest of you stay here. Don't let anyone in.' Then he turned to Coates. 'Let's see who we're up against.'

That man favoured him with a half-smile. 'If I had a shiny gold Double Eagle for every time you've said that, I'd be richer than John D. Rockefeller!'

* * *

The saloon's interior appeared exceptionally spacious, doubtless because it was practically deserted. Its only apparent occupants were two men behind the bar, but they definitely weren't selling drinks. Both wore blue tunics, and one of them, a tall bearded individual sporting captain's bars on his shoulder straps, held a sawn-off shotgun cocked and ready. The younger, enlisted man had a Springfield Carbine resting on the counter, pointing at the entrance. Although there were no customers, the tables and chairs had been deliberately left scattered around the floor, so as to hinder any sudden rush.

Tucker and Coates closed the door behind them, but made no attempt to advance. As usual, it was the former who had the words. 'That doesn't look like a regulation issue firearm,' he remarked conversationally, glancing meaningfully at Harris's twelve-gauge.

The officer responded brusquely. 'I'll

use anything that comes to hand.'

Tucker nodded, as though everything was suddenly plain to him. 'Is that so? Well, we're here on behalf of the Secretary of the Interior. I'm told that you've got someone who belongs to him. So if you'll just hand the cuss over, we'll be on our way and you won't need to use that crowd-pleaser. How's that sound?'

'It sounds like you're trying to do me a favour.'

'Oh, we are,' Tucker agreed smoothly. 'We most definitely are.'

Harris locked eyes with the spokesman. His palms were suddenly sweaty, and there was a nervous flutter in his belly. His time in the army hadn't provided any experience of facing down hired guns, but he'd be damned if that was going to stop him. 'I answer only to General Sheridan, Commanding General of the United States Army. I have placed this building under martial law. Anyone who might happen to be in it is under my protection. So if you fellas intend on staying, you need to surrender all your weapons.'

That was too much for Coates. 'We don't hand our guns over to anybody!'

The soldier shrugged, 'Well, in that case, you need to back out onto the street . . . and stay there.'

Tucker didn't move. He just maintained his hard stare. 'Now that really ain't very friendly of you, Captain. The least you could do is offer us a drink.'

Harris lowered his shotgun abruptly so that its muzzles were now pointing directly at the two men. 'Bar's closed. Now git. And if you come back in here toting any firearms, I'll kill you both!'

For maybe a full minute, there was no movement of any kind. Then, finally, Brett Tucker sighed with annoyance and glanced at his companion. He jerked his head slightly, and then the two men turned away. 'We'll be seeing you, Captain,' he called over his shoulder as they left the building.

As the door closed behind them, it was the officer's turn to sigh. Still keeping his shotgun levelled, he took a step back

193

and glanced down at his prisoner. 'You hear all that? And there's more of them outside. They haven't come here to dust you off and buy you a drink. They want you dead or alive, but dead's more likely because they're killers for sure.'

Manacled to one of the counter's support struts, Tatum's freedom of movement was very limited. 'So maybe you should take these damned irons off of me and give me a gun.'

'No deal,' Harris retorted. 'I like you better down there.'

'What if they torch the place? I could burn to death.'

The captain smiled at Private Price as he replied. 'By all accounts, you'd deserve it, after what you did to Lomax!'

★ ★ ★

'Seems like that soldier boy's looking for a promotion,' Jim Coates remarked, as they rejoined the others on the street.

'Then we'll just have to make sure he doesn't live that long,' Tucker barked.

'That shit-faced marshal said there were three of them. I only counted two, an' maybe their prisoner down behind the bar. What's round the back?'

'One door, bolted from the inside,' reported one of those sent to look.

'Uh-huh.' Peering around, Tucker spotted Bruns and Kruntz's Hardware Store a short distance away. A number of citizens were observing curiously through the window. 'Take yourself over there and get a couple of kerosene lamps. And pay for them. We might kill folks, but we ain't thieves!' As that man hurried off to do his bidding, he continued. 'We'll burn the sons of bitches out. And if nobody survives, well then so much the better!'

11

The Tenth Day — Afternoon

'So that's how it's to be!' Harris's voice was harsh and strained. Through a window, he had just spotted Tucker's men adjusting the wicks on two oil lamps.

'Shall we rush them, sir?' Price was young and eager, like a rutting buck. But the time for heroics was already gone, if it had ever existed, because his commander then saw two men in full flow.

'Get down, Private, if you value your skin!'

A moment later, the glass was completely shattered as both incendiaries were hurled through it. The kerosene-filled lamps hit the wooden floor and exploded in bursts of flame. Then a volley of shots rang out, and hot lead slammed into the solid counter. Their attackers had little expectation of hitting anyone. They just wanted to prevent the soldiers from fighting the fires before they took hold.

It worked.

'They know their business, I'll grant them that,' the captain exclaimed.

A howl of protest came from near their feet. 'You goddamn tin soldier. You can't leave me here to burn!'

The two men temporarily ignored Tatum. With flames spreading rapidly to the cheap wooden furniture, they had more pressing concerns, because it was obvious that the saloon was doomed.

'Mister White sure ain't gonna like this,' Harris couldn't resist remarking, in a parody of Bob the bartender. Then to Price, he ordered, 'Release him from there, but keep his arms fastened behind his back.' Even as he spoke, he placed the shotgun muzzles against Tatum's skull. 'Don't even think about giving him any trouble. Whatever happens here, you're still my prisoner.'

By the time Price had complied, even the walls were burning, and the heat was growing in intensity. It was time to retreat.

'Keep your heads down and move into

the back room,' Harris ordered.

Behind the bar, at the rear of the saloon, was a small storeroom with a single door leading outside. With only a flimsy dividing wall, this wouldn't be a haven for long, and beyond that the open thoroughfare awaited them. Doubtless it was here that the trap would be sprung.

★ ★ ★

Brett Tucker observed the proceedings with professional detachment. His men had ceased firing because, as expected, the flames had taken irrevocable hold on the wooden structure. So far so good.

'Jim, how's about taking three men around the back? Catch those blue bellies if they decide to high tail it. And remember, there's likely another one of them on the loose somewheres!'

Coates wordlessly flipped a salute, and then led his chosen followers down the side of the burning building. On reaching the rear, three of them spread out and trained their weapons on the back door. One held a twelve-gauge that would surely tear to pieces anyone who dared to emerge. Their leader chose to carefully scan the surrounding buildings. The whole town appeared to be deserted, with the citizens wisely giving the violent confrontation a wide berth. The possible whereabouts of a third man was an unpleasant niggle in his craw . . . if he even existed. If it turned out that such was just a spiteful invention of the marshal, then that son of a bitch would surely suffer for it.

★   ★   ★

Unsurprisingly, the dividing wall had proven to be an illusory barrier. The frail timbers were already alight, and the punishing heat would soon become unbearable. Moses Harris glanced at the bolted rear door, and regretfully decided that the moment had come.

'Get those bolts back, Private,' he commanded. 'But don't open it 'til I say.' As Price obeyed, the captain glanced at

199

Tatum. 'Get your face to the floor if you know what's good for you.'

The assassin had sense enough not to argue and soon lay with his arms secured behind his back, like a stranded fish. Then, with a rending crash, the thin wall collapsed and there was a tremendous rush of superheated air. If they were to stay in the building much longer, they would surely end up like Ben Lomax. The three men had no option other than to take their chances outside, and trust to Deke Wilson's lethal abilities.

'OK,' Harris said. 'Open that door, but stay out of sight.'

As the door swung back on creaking hinges, Price dropped to the floor, but the expected fusillade never came. Instead there was merely the eerie silence of an empty street, which only seemed to highlight the crackling of burning timbers behind them.

'Clever,' Harris muttered. Their assailants desired to draw them out into the open, and with the spreading inferno they would soon get their wish. 'You'd

better be out there somewhere, Deke!'
was his fervent prayer.

★　★　★

The army scout was indeed *out there*.
Using a wooden barrel as leverage, he
had climbed quietly onto the sloping roof
of a conveniently empty cabin that faced
onto the rear of the blazing saloon. His
position afforded him a grandstand view
of the spectacularly condemned structure. And since he was on the reverse
slope, he had been able to remain hidden from the four gun thugs lying in
wait somewhere below. Now, as Private
Price opened the back door gingerly,
these men were about to get the surprise
of their brutalized lives.

Drawing deeply on a Daniel Webster
cigar that he had been saving for a special
occasion, Wilson touched the glowing
end to the short black fuse protruding
from a single stick of dynamite. As the
black powder-impregnated cord flared
into life, he shuffled further up the roof.

From listening to their movements, he had a fair idea where two of the gunmen were, and that would have to do. Waiting until the fuse had almost burned down, he lobbed the explosive stick out and to the side. Even as it touched down in the slush, Wilson grabbed his Sharps and got to his knees.

* * *

Jim Coates caught sight of the relatively small object out of the corner of his eye. With sparks flying from it, no great intellect was required to realize that trouble was coming.

'Get down, all of you!' he bellowed, but it was too late. At such close quarters, the shock wave created by the massive explosion was quite literally ear splitting. One man caught the full brunt of it, and was thrown from his feet with blood streaming from his ears and nose. As a cascade of muddy water rained down on his comrades, they tried to work out just what had occurred.

Coates had sense enough to stay in the cloying mud, but the other two survivors could think only of escape. Associating the buildings with hidden danger, they ran out into the street, which was exactly what Wilson had anticipated. Rapidly taking aim between a pair of narrow shoulders, he triggered his buffalo gun. Its heavy piece of lead punched a hole straight through his victim's body. Distorted by internal impact, the bullet took chunks of bone and gristle with it as it then travelled on into the disintegrating saloon. The sheer momentum behind the projectile thrust the helpless gun thug forward into the slush. He was dead before he hit the ground.

* * *

Brett Tucker had just concluded that it was time to move his men around to the rear of the saloon, since there was no longer the remotest possibility of anyone escaping through the front. The muffled explosion, followed by the sound of a high-powered rifle, reinforced that belief urgently. Those sounds could mean only one thing . . . the third man.

'Get over there!' he yelled. 'You see anyone you don't know, kill him! And check the roofs.'

Winchesters at the ready, his three men set off cautiously, keeping well clear of the fierce heat. Tucker was no fool. Following on behind, he made damn sure they were between him and any likely foe.

* * *

Moses Harris believed in leading from the front, and so he was first out of the saloon's back door. His rush into the street coincided with Wilson claiming his second victim. The only man left standing was a professional and very capable hired gun, but the tremendous explosion followed by the death of his companion had unsettled him. It was that which gave the captain the slight edge, and that was all he required. As he saw his sole opponent desperately swing a Winchester towards him, Harris discharged both barrels of his sawn-off in that man's direction.

The jarring recoil and cloud of powder smoke meant that he didn't immediately see the lethal damage that he'd caused. Yet that didn't matter, because damage there was aplenty! The relentless, high-pitched screaming confirmed that. Much of the spread of lead shot had struck the gun thug's face and upper torso, tearing bloody pieces of flesh from his features. As he dropped to his knees, pawing at his eyes, it was obvious that he would be neither threat nor even use to anyone ever again.

Even as Private Price and his prisoner emerged from the dreadful heat, Harris abruptly saw his scout on top of a nearby roof. 'Get off the damn street, Captain!' that man yelled. 'Rest of them's coming.' With that, he extracted another stick of dynamite from his pocket.

★ ★ ★

It was because Tucker had lagged behind his men that he spotted the stranger on the roof. The son of a bitch was in the process of hurling something in their direction. Reacting with practised speed, he swung his Winchester on track and fired just as his target let go of the dynamite.

An instant earlier and Wilson would have been blown to pieces by his own explosive device. As it was, he took a bullet in his right side that punched him backwards. In great pain and helplessly off balance, he dropped his rifle and then fell straight off the roof. The hissing red stick continued on its trajectory, but this time the second group saw it coming and dived for cover. The terrific blast that followed threw up a great deal of muck, but injured no one.

★ ★ ★

As Harris saw his scout disappear from sight, his heart sank. Somehow, it had never occurred to him that one of them might actually get killed. Forcing himself to think rationally, the officer knew that they had to get across the street whilst their opponents were still sheltering from the blast. The gun thugs couldn't yet be sure that there weren't more to come.

'Run for it, Price!' he hollered.

Tatum, realizing full well that he was also in the line of fire, offered no resistance, and soon the three of them were moving down the side of Wilson's cabin. Harris paused long enough to reload his shotgun. 'Check on Deke,' he ordered. 'I'll hold them off.'

★ ★ ★

Two of their men were dead, whilst a third, still screaming his lungs out further down the street, might just as well have been.

Coates, whose clothing was now covered in mud, glanced sourly over at his partner. 'This could have gone better,' he muttered.

'*We're* still alive, ain't we?' the other

man retorted sharply. Brett Tucker was boiling mad, but he knew better than to let his emotions run reckless. He took a deep breath, before addressing all the survivors. 'Listen up, all of you. I want every mother's son of them dead. No prisoners. Savvy? Now spread out, but keep each other in sight.' With that, he cautiously headed for the cabin that Wilson had fallen from. All thoughts of hanging back had left him.

The others did as instructed, and so when the muzzles of a shotgun poked around the corner, there were no longer any juicy targets, only five individuals with strung out nerves and itchy trigger fingers. Four Winchesters and a shotgun crashed out, almost in unison, their projectiles carving out chunks of wood from the building.

★ ★ ★

Recognizing that he was well and truly outgunned, Moses Harris didn't even attempt to take aim. He merely returned fire for effect, and then hurried off to find the others. What he discovered was distressing. Deke Wilson's coat was soaked with blood, and he was clearly in great pain.

Tatum, whilst secretly gloating at the scout's downfall, also had something else on his mind. 'I'll allow you've done all right so far, but you ain't gonna catch those fellas with any more sucker punches. They're hurting now, an' they'll be ready for you. So take these irons off, give me a gun, an' we'll call it quits.'

Harris shook his head emphatically. 'I don't do deals with assassins. You're my prisoner, and that's what you'll stay!'

Tatum's features became suffused with blood. 'God damn it all to hell! You really are one stubborn son of a bitch!'

Completely dismissing him, the officer turned to his scout. Concern was etched on his face. 'How goes it, Deke?'

That man *just* managed a smile. He was hurting real bad, but there really was no time to tend to his wound. 'I'll survive, Captain. But we need to get under cover. I've stashed the Remington in that shed over yonder. There's a mighty big engine in there, so even if they try burning us out again we'll have some protection. Lend me an arm, and let's go.'

Together, with Harris assisting Wilson, and Price prodding a very reluctant captive, they all hurried over to their new holdout position. The huge shed was situated towards the edge of town at the end of a spur line. Inside, a number of Northern Pacific employees were servicing what was indeed a massive engine, prior to its ascent of the Bozeman Pass. Considering the amount of violence that had occurred only a short distance away, it was amazing that they were still working. As it was, they looked on with suspicion as the four men, one of them quite obviously badly wounded, appeared before them. The officer made damn sure that, before saying his piece, all the workmen saw his army tunic.

'I'm Captain Harris, 1st Cavalry,' he began. 'You likely heard the shooting, and you sure couldn't have missed the explosions. There's been some killings, and there will be more. So it would behove you all to hightail it out of here.'

As though reinforcing his words, a bullet slammed into the outside wall behind the new arrivals. The railroad men needed no further telling. Dropping their tools, they left . . . fast! With a groan of pain, Wilson leaned against the side of the engine, and gestured over to where he had stashed the Remington.

'For what it's worth, you might as well use it, Captain, but I think we're a mite overmatched. It's a fine gun for sure at long range, but it can't hope to match their Winchesters for speed. Same goes for your Springfield,' he added, glancing over at Price. As though emphasizing that very fact, Tucker's men opened up from various positions around the shed.

Seemingly still wary of the dynamite, it was obvious that the gunmen were trying to make a point because the hot lead came thick and fast. Splinters flew everywhere, and some of the bullets even managed to penetrate the thin walls. Shotgun blasts mingled with repeating fire. The noise was deafening, and it wasn't until some of their opponents had to reload that Wilson was able to have his say.

'Up in that cab, we might be safe for a while, but sooner or later they'll likely plug one of us. An' if they fire the place, we *could* maybe survive, but we're always gonna be on the back foot.'

Harris stared at him intently. He knew there was more to come. 'So what are you thinking on, Deke?'

That man favoured him with a sad smile. His face was pale and waxy. 'I'm done for, Captain, but I can still pull a trigger . . . *and* light a fuse. Get me up in that cab, with the sawn-off and dynamite, an' I'll whittle those bastards down a bit. All you've got to do is let them see four of you clear out of here. They'll have seen my blood in the snow, an' know that one of us is wounded. Get this big coat off of me an' hold it low. They'll think you're dragging me.' He paused for a moment, and offered a wan smile. 'What do you think to my plan?'

Harris grimaced. 'I like it, except for the fact that it means leaving you behind.'

'Happen it's for the best. Call it payback for all my bad deeds.'

The soldier shook his head. 'I've only ever seen *good* deeds from you, Deke Wilson.'

A cloud seemed to sweep across that man's pained features, as though he had suddenly been assailed by distant memories. 'Yeah, well. You didn't know me back in the day!'

★ ★ ★

'Those cockchafers are on the move again,' Coates bellowed at Tucker. 'All of them, looks like, going full chisel.' He had just finished feeding fresh cartridges through the loading gate of his Winchester, and had spotted what seemed to be four figures fleeing along the side of the spur line. One of them appeared to be in a bad way, because it took two others to

213

half carry him. Considering the amount of fresh blood leading to the shed, that all seemed perfectly reasonable.

Tucker, his view obscured by the vast structure, had to take his word for it, but he was by nature suspicious. 'All four? Are you sure?'

Coates glared over at him with annoyance. There were times when his partner really overplayed the leadership role. 'Damn right, I'm sure. I just said so, didn't I? Take a look see if you don't believe me!'

'No need to get wrathy,' Tucker yelled back. 'Use the building as cover.'

'Yeah, yeah,' Coates muttered. After nodding at those nearest to him, he suddenly broke into a sprint, veering off to the right so that he would have the shed between him and the fugitives. Fear gave him speed. He had seen his man felled by the buffalo gun earlier. It was as though the poor bastard had actually been struck by one of those huge shagies. Zigzagging awkwardly in the slush, he was aware that the others were at least following him. His breath was running ragged by the time he slammed to a stop against the timber wall. As Tucker and their three remaining men joined him, Coates sucked in great drafts of chill air. His feet were cold, he was still blathered in mud, and he'd definitely had enough of this running shit.

Brett Tucker took a calculated gamble and stuck his head around the huge open door. The only thing in sight was the silent engine facing him, and its tender, just visible at the rear. Any workmen were understandably absent, and of course their antagonists had all fled. Winchester at the ready, he stepped out into the open and waited. As expected, nothing happened.

Coates and the others joined him. 'See, I told you they'd cleared out,' that man remarked huffily.

Tucker's temper wasn't improving any. What should have been a simple arrest had already likely cost them three dead, and was now turning into a lethal game of cat and mouse. 'Let's move,' he barked, and headed off down the side of the engine, followed by the others. It was only then that he caught the faint whiff of tobacco smoke.

* * *

Deke Wilson knew without any doubt that he was dying. Otherwise, how come he wasn't enjoying his expensive cigar? His long johns were sticky with blood, and the slightest movement hurt like hell. Then he heard voices, and suddenly none of it mattered anymore. He was sitting in the cab with his back wedged against the back wall. In his right hand was the cocked sawn-off. In the left was a stick of dynamite. Very clearly, he heard, 'Let's move,' in a seemingly angry tone. It was time.

Sucking weakly on the cigar, he just managed to get the end glowing. Touching the short, black fuse to it, he sighed with relief as it burst into life. Footsteps came closer, until suddenly some unknown gun thug appeared by the steps that led up into the cab. The man's eyes widened at the horrific sight before him, and desperately he swung his rifle over.

'Catch,' said Wilson lightly, as he tossed the explosive stick through the opening.

'Oh, Jesus!' the other man howled, and disappeared abruptly from sight.

Almost immediately there was an awesome detonation just beyond the cab walls, which left the scout's ears ringing painfully. Mud, blood, and a piece of charred flesh splattered over his already bloodied frontage. Agonised screams echoed around the shed's interior. With a supreme effort, Wilson levered himself away from the wall, so that he fell forward across the cab floor. A fresh wave of pain swept over him, but by sheer will-power he managed to poke the shotgun's stubby barrels outside. The devastation that he saw should have provided much satisfaction, but he was just too far-gone to do anything but squeeze the triggers. A lethal spread of lead shot added to the existing carnage, and abruptly no one was screaming anymore. He smiled and finally allowed his eyes to close. Whatever happened now just didn't matter a damn!

★ ★ ★

Moses Harris winced as the explosion rent the air. He could only imagine what had happened in that engine shed. Then he heard the twin discharge of the twelve-gauge, and he knew what he had to do. Clutching the Remington, he commanded, 'Stay with this son of a bitch. Whatever happens, don't come looking.'

Private Price nodded reluctantly. 'Yes, sir,' he acknowledged, and then his officer was gone.

'Get these bastard irons off of me, soldier!' Tatum demanded, knowing that this was his best and probably only chance. 'If he gets kilt, I'm the best hope you've got of surviving all this.'

The enlisted man glared at him angrily. He was sick of taking orders as it was without having to listen to this murdering wretch. 'This is for Lane Turner,' he remarked, as he smashed the butt of his Springfield into the side of Tatum's skull. That luckless individual fell sideways without a sound, but thankfully he was still breathing.

Unaware of the violent occurrence behind him, Harris first arced off to his right, so as to approach the shed from a direction hopefully unexpected by any survivors in it. So it was that he witnessed Deke Wilson's final moment. Of their pursuers, only two remained on their feet. One of them, whom he recognized as Tucker, appeared to be helplessly dazed and witless. Favouring his left arm, he stumbled aimlessly about. The other man, Coates, appeared both unhurt and dangerous, because at that instant he unleashed a rapid fire from his carbine at close range into the cab.

Raw anger coursed through the captain, and he raised the Remington to his shoulder. He was unfamiliar with the powerful rifle, but hell, a gun was a gun, and at such range the sights couldn't be anything other than honest. He knew that, by rights, as an officer and gentleman, he should really attempt to arrest the son of a bitch, but his only desire was to kill him.

Thumbing back the hammer, he aimed directly at Coates. That man had literally emptied his weapon at Deke. Now, as he stood in a cloud of smoke, some sixth sense prompted him to turn just at the moment Harris fired. The bullet struck him in his left shoulder with enough force to knock him clean off his feet.

The soldier opened the rolling block breech to replace the cartridge, and then advanced purposefully. As he drew closer, he could hear Tucker repetitively mumbling, 'I can't see. I can't see.' Too bad for him, he decided!

Jim Coates writhed on the ground, cursing his bad luck. And it was only going to get worse. Looking up, he saw the grim-faced soldier level the Remington at his face. 'I was only doing my job. I don't deserve this,' he protested.

'Neither did Deke,' came the chilling

response, and then the hammer dropped with terrible results. As the smoke cleared, Harris surveyed the gruesome mess that had once been a human being. He blinked rapidly, and his hands began to tremble. He'd never executed anyone in cold blood before, and he decided there and then that he never would again . . . even if it meant resigning his commission and clerking in a hardware store or some such!

Epilogue

The Eleventh Day

The two disconsolate men, both suffering from a variety of minor injuries, were manacled together and confined in Devereaux's jailhouse. The marshal, of course, had had no say in the arrests or subsequent imprisonment, but he was gaining a certain puerile pleasure out of needling them.

'Tatum and Tucker. That has quite a ring to it,' he crowed. 'Maybe you ought to go into business together.'

Tatum, his head bruised and still aching from the previous afternoon, regarded him with malevolent silence. The more lucid Tucker, who had recovered his sight after the dynamite flash, preferred to respond in kind. 'And maybe you should stick your suggestions where the sun don't shine, Marshal.' His retort was suddenly highlighted by the shrill scream of a steam whistle, announcing

222

the arrival of the eleven-thirty train from Columbus.

Devereaux chuckled. He'd just thought of another good one. 'Looks to me like you're both plumb chained to your work ... Hee hee.'

* * *

It was a short time later that the tramp of many boots could be heard on the wooden sidewalk. The jailhouse door swung open and a seeming flood of blue uniforms poured into the outer office.

'Christ!' exclaimed Devereaux. 'Livingston's been invaded.'

Moses Harris regarded him pityingly. 'This is Major Smith. He's come to remove your prisoners. Then we'll all be leaving you shortly, Marshal. You'll get your town back. With the exception of Frank White's, of course.'

The lawman's expression was far from jubilant. 'There's an awful lot of people pissed off about what you did to their saloon.'

The captain shrugged. 'Tell Bob I'm sorry.' Then he paused, as though puzzled by something. 'Where is he, anyway?'

'Left town. Took the three-thirty eastbound yesterday afternoon. Guess he figured on reporting to his boss personally.'

Harris chuckled dryly and pointed at the disconsolate figure of Brett Tucker. 'Well, that son of a bitch was actually responsible. And your hardware store sold him the makings. But if anyone really wants to come looking for me, I'll be in Mammoth, where I belong.' Then, losing interest in the profitless conversation, he turned to Sheridan's staff officer, who had been listening to the exchange with detached amusement. 'What will happen to these two, sir?'

The major glanced over at the cell. 'That's up to the general. As you probably know, he can be one tough and prickly *hombre* when he's in the mood, which is most of the time. Both of them are responsible for the deaths of serving soldiers, so I reckon they'll hang together!'

Both Tatum and Tucker were hardened thugs in their own way, but neither could disguise certain uneasiness at that disclosure. That didn't go unnoticed by Captain Harris, who nodded grimly. It was at his strenuous insistence that Smith had agreed to classify the civilian scout, Deke Wilson, in the category of soldier. It had been the least he could do for him!

* * *

Secretary Lamar could feel the sweat forming uncomfortably in his armpits. He wasn't used to being kept waiting, and the experience didn't sit well with him. The cabinet officer was seated at his usual table in Mades' Restaurant, awaiting the arrival of the financier, Jay Cooke. It was highly unusual for that individual to be late for anything. And after all, it was the financier who had sent the message urgently requesting this meeting with the Secretary of the Interior!

As he feverishly pondered the possible ramifications behind such an appeal, Lamar glanced over at the foyer for perhaps the fifth time since his arrival. What he saw almost made him choke. A short, heavily built figure wearing the blue uniform of a lieutenant general was staring directly at him. Philip Henry Sheridan, with his distinctive drooping moustache, had put on a great deal of weight since his glory days in the late war, but there could still be no doubting his aggressive determination. As he strode purposefully over to his prey, there was a steely glint in the commanding general's eyes that surely boded ill.

Somewhat shakily, Lamar got to his feet, and bowed slightly to the approaching figure. 'General Sheridan,' he croaked. 'This is an unexpected pleasure.'

That man didn't bother himself with any unnecessary civilities. 'Sit down, you snake, before I knock you down in front of all these good people!'

The Secretary's eyes widened like

saucers. He wondered briefly whether to attempt some bluster in his defence, but then recalled that the soldier had doubtless personally killed men in his time. Meekly, he did as instructed. Somehow, he had an idea what was coming.

'Unquestionably, you were expecting that scoundrel, Cooke,' Sheridan began in his typically forthright manner. 'Well, I've already told him what I'm going to tell you, and he had the sense to accept it. Your avaricious and murderous game has run its course, Mister Secretary! I've received a telegram from one of my staff officers confirming that he has taken over custody of two men held by a certain Captain Harris. I believe you've been in correspondence with him in his capacity as Superintendent of Yellowstone Park. A good man that Harris, worthy of promotion. Anyway, one of the prisoners is called Tucker. Brett Tucker. I understand that he works for you.'

Lamar suddenly felt his heart racing unpleasantly. As his palms grew sweaty, he haltingly asked, 'What is it that you want of me, general?'

Sheridan favoured him with a cold smile. 'Withdraw! Cease any and all activities relating to the extension of the Northern Pacific Railroad and the intended transportation of silver across the Yellowstone National Park. An Act of Congress created it, with the intention of preserving everything in it for future generations. Greed has no place there.'

Somehow, Lamar knew there was more to come. 'And?'

'Resign from the government immediately. If you do, you won't end up in court. And believe me, after what's happened out there, you're getting off lightly.'

The Secretary made a small show of thinking it over, but he knew he had no choice. Tentatively, he reached out his right hand. 'Agreed.'

General Sheridan subjected him to a bone-crushing handshake, and then grimaced. 'Those are some real clammy hands you've got there. You're like the few buffalo left in Yellowstone, Mister

Secretary. Obsolete . . . only *they* didn't deserve to end up like that!'

We do hope that you have enjoyed reading this large print book.

Did you know that all of our titles are available for purchase?

We publish a wide range of high quality large print books including:
Romances, Mysteries, Classics
General Fiction
Non Fiction and Westerns

Special interest titles available in large print are:
The Little Oxford Dictionary
Music Book, Song Book
Hymn Book, Service Book

Also available from us courtesy of Oxford University Press:
Young Readers' Dictionary
(large print edition)
Young Readers' Thesaurus
(large print edition)

For further information or a free brochure, please contact us at:
Ulverscroft Large Print Books Ltd.,
The Green, Bradgate Road, Anstey,
Leicester, LE7 7FU, England.
Tel: (00 44) 0116 236 4325
Fax: (00 44) 0116 234 0205

Other titles in the
Linford Western Library:

TWO TREES HOLLOW

Frank Chandler

Sweetspring is a quiet town . . . until an itinerant gang of robbers causes havoc. Wesley Vernon, a mine engineer, thinks he recognizes their leader as a childhood friend, and determines to bring him to justice. But before he sets off he is devastated to learn that his intended bride, Maddy, has been promised to a wealthy banker from Boston. Never could Wes have imagined how his moral courage would be tested as he faces gun battles, bank raids, and a prison breakout . . .